Charles A. Turek

THE STEAM LOCOMOTIVE MURDERS

A Charlie Komensky Novel

PAGINATION

Pagination Books, Albuquerque, NM, U.S.A.

This novel is a work of fiction. All characters, people, places, events, and organizations are a product of the author's imagination. Any similarity to real people, places, events or organizations is strictly coincidental, with the exception of background historical facts.

ISBN-13: 978-0615864587
ISBN-10: 0615864589

THE STEAM LOCOMOTIVE MURDERS

A CHARLIE KOMENSKY MYSTERY
BY CHARLES A. TUREK

Also by Charles A. Turek

Charlie Komensky Series
The Flat Tire Murders
Wheel Deadly – short story

Timemapper Series
The Acceleration of Time

Novels
A Tunnel Too Far
The Plutonium Standard

Chapter One

The weather was too good. The Sunday sun hadn't yet broken over the high peaks of the Rocky Mountains, but the northern New Mexico sky had already turned a full, almost cloudless blue. *Cielo azul.* Only thin wisps of ice-crystal clouds brushed the highest peaks as the light wind found its way over the Sangre de Christos and the San Juans. The crisp weather of an early fall day would be great for the tourist business; cold in the morning, but, by noon, mild enough to see everyone in shirtsleeves. Stuff just seemed to go wrong every time the weather was too good. Mike believed in omens, and, although a devout Catholic, thought there was something to the idea that the old, pagan gods still roamed the northern mountains. As a result, he couldn't shake the feeling that something would go wrong.

Mike Ortega had been running the narrow-gauge tourist railroad for almost fifteen years, and his pulse never failed to quicken at the prospect of running an antique steam locomotive over the high mountain pass on a day like this. He told himself to get a grip and enjoy the day. He'd be closing out the season in three weeks, and, with his name on the schedule for weekend runs only, he would only have a few more opportunities like this before snow, already sticking at the highest elevations, made the pass too costly for the tourist line to run over. Mike liked the winters as well as the other seasons, but an old steam locomotive pulling a train and pushing a ton of snow off the tracks ahead of it burned up too much fuel—and fuel meant money—to allow the line the luxury of operating during winter months. Sure, people would come to see it, and even to ride, but then, too, there were the dangers of frostbite and an extreme form of altitude sickness that seemed to plague winter passengers. There would be only one run over the pass this winter, the week between Christmas and New Years, and that would be all the insurance company would allow without a substantial bump in liability premiums. He wished the insurance companies and the lawyers didn't exist, but they were reality, a necessary evil, in this era when anything that went wrong was somebody else's fault.

Short and overweight, but not grossly so, Mike Ortega wore a light flannel jacket over his engineer's bib overalls to cut the morning chill. He chose not to wear a hat, as his thick, curly black hair provided adequate warmth for his head. Besides, once on the premises, he was supposed to be wearing a hard hat and vest, both of which he would put on soon in due time, before anybody who could criticize him came on duty. Mike's heritage was Northern New Mexico Hispanic on his father's side, and Celtic on his mother's, so except for the black hair, he could have passed for an engineman on any railroad in the east or deep south. His green eyes came from his mother, and he used them, along with his handsome, jovial appearance, to charm the girls, Northern New Mexico and otherwise.

Mike sighed at the thought of having to let the three operating steam locomotives in the railroad's fleet go cold for the winter. There was something about a fired-up steam locomotive that made it a living, monstrously large beast of burden, but a beast with a character and a personality. No. 1 in the fleet, for instance, was a beast with eight driving wheels*.

*See Charlie's Steam Locomotive Glossary at end of book.

Re-numbered from 435, a number she had carried for its original owner long since absorbed into one of the larger railroad systems of today, No. 1 had been built by Baldwin Locomotive Works in 1925 and was undoubtedly his favorite locomotive. It seemed to Mike that, the older the locomotive, the easier it was to become familiar with her temperament. One spot had been given various names throughout its almost century-old career. As was the habit of railroads in designating their equipment, she had been given a designation consisting of a letter and number that stuck to this day. K-36. The letter presumably put it into the group of all locomotives belonging to the Denver and Rio Grande Railroad, built to the same specifications and having the wheel arrangement consisting of a single non-powered axle leading, four powered axles, and a single axle trailing. This had become a very popular wheel arrangement for the hauling of freight, and gained the nickname "Mikado" for reasons that Mike could explain to tourist groups but didn't fully agree with. Far from being like anything Asian, these locomotives were purely American machines bred by American industry in the early 20th Century. "Empress maybe, but not Mikado," thought Mike.

Whether or not he understood her name, she was a massive beast with whom Mike had an understanding. He would put up with her faults and would not swear at her if she would continue to run when he needed her to and not blow up and kill him when he was running her. Not that an explosion was likely, or even more probable than your car engine blowing up on the highway. It's just that, with a hundred ninety-five pounds of superheated steam inside a teakettle that old, given the heat, smoke and cinders generated, you had to wonder if you would one day be riding her straight into hell.

The small railroad yard was laid out parallel to the main road through town, which limited the town's business district—including a hotel, two Laundromats, three restaurants, an everything's a dollar store, three gas station-convenience store combos, one package liquor store, and a medical clinic—to the west side of the road. The combination of brick and frame storefronts, some with false facades, and a few frame residences, gave Agua Rojo, New Mexico, the look of a western cowboy town. Locomotive No.1 stood on the ready track outside the small engine house and threw a mighty, early morning shadow all the way across the road to the footings of the storefronts. At 7,386 feet elevation, the shadows were so well defined that Mike could make out shadow details like the thin wires leading from the steam turbine generator to the top of the firebox.

As he stood in the shade of the big engine, Mike looked back along her tender to where No. 3 simmered. The hostler—a term for a man who tended the locomotives to see that they were ready for running the next day's trains—still tended the fire and watched the gauges on No. 3 as she built up steam. No. 3 would go out on the second train of the day, which left about an hour and a half after the first. Behind No. 3, Mike could see the outline of No. 4, parked and already cold for the season. For reasons long lost in history, there had never been a No. 2 on this railroad.

Mike walked around the engine looking for anything that might be wrong. The hostler would have checked her over and lubricated the important places with an Alemite gun or oil can, and probably done everything but pat her flanks as if she were a real horse and not an iron one, but it would be Mike's responsibility as "engineer" to see to it that the locomotive was safe to pull a train full of passengers up the mountain. Black except for silver lettering and a silvery coating of leaded paint over the smokebox, the locomotive made it hard for anyone to see into the many rods and links underneath that made up the undercarriage and suspension for the eight wheels that were linked to each other, and to the main rods and valve gear rods that were part of the steam engine itself. Because this was a three-foot gauge locomotive—the standard is four feet eight and a half inches—the wheels sat inside the frame and actually made it easier to lubricate main bearings. But all of the rods and counterweights were on the outside, giving these narrow gauge locomotives , when running at full throttle, the appearance of walking down the main line on their rods and cranks without benefit of wheels.

But she could pull—Lordy could she pull. The thrill of hauling out on the throttle and feeling these ladies, these creatures, surge forward and walk up the mountain with a train of cars was almost sexual. It was what got Mike up mornings.

Mike exhaled, took in a deep breath of mountain air scented with lube oil and coal smoke, and walked around to the sunny side of the locomotive. As he did so, he glanced back towards No. 3, now steaming mightily with its blower on full to create enough draft to create more steam to make more heat and enough steam to get her up to her operating pressure. Her hostler was still on the ground oiling the machinery and paying no attention to Mike. The sun reflected off the huge clouds of coal smoke coming from No. 3, and, from this angle, there appeared to be wisps of grey smoke coming from No. 4. Mike blinked his eyes to clear them of tears—the bright, unfiltered mountain sunlight always made his eyes water if he tried to look at anything for too long, even with sunglasses. Blinking and looking again, he still saw smoke over No. 4. "Henry!" he yelled to the hostler.

It was no surprise to Mike that Henry didn't hear him. Henry focused on his work and stood much too close to the rumble of the coal fire, the grind of the stoker, the whine of the turbo-generator and the thumping of the cross-compound air pumps to hear. Sure of what he saw, Mike ran towards Henry. "Henry! Henry!" Had the hostler made a mistake or fired up No. 4 for some other reason? Mike didn't want a situation on his hands before the season was over.

Henry looked up at his boss without removing the nozzle of the oil can from its place in an oil sump on one of the main bearings. Eschewing the traditional blue denim bibs for an orange set of full coveralls, he wore the requisite orange hardhat and looked every bit the professional railroader. His eyes twinkled in his dark-skinned face of typically African-American features—though his mother was a Native American Zuni—and , at a foot taller than his boss, Henry looked down on Mike. "What's got you so all riled up?"

"Did you fire up Four?" Mike panted and bent to put his hands on his knees to catch his breath. The run in the high atmosphere wouldn't have been his first choice for morning exercise.

"Now how could I do that?" asked Henry, still not concerned or stopping his task of oiling around No. 3. "We took the grate out for welding yesterday. Ain't no grate in that firebox!"

"Well, she's smoking."

This got Henry to glance back to Number Four, but he still continued his oiling. "Probably just secondary smoke," he observed. "The wind is gettin' into the open firebox and blowin' soot up and out the flues. These girls get themselves pretty dirty in a season's runnin' up and down the mountain."

Mike stood up full and pulled a long breath. "Henry, you may be right, but that seems like too much smoke to me. Let's investigate."

The hostler grudgingly propped his oil can on a rod that was more or less level and followed Mike as the latter walked back around and past No. 3's tender. "Can't have no fire in the firebox," he mumbled to himself.

Both men stopped alongside the locomotive's pilot and started up at the stack, probably eight feet above their heads on the smudged silver nose of the machine. "That sure looks like smoke to me," stated Mike.

Without being asked to do it, Henry grabbed a handrail and swung himself up onto the narrow pilot deck. The door on the front of the smokebox of this engine was elongated, circular in shape at the top and bottom, but otherwise rectangular, and hinged near the center of the circular front of the smokebox. This practice was peculiar to some steam locomotives that had other equipment, like pumps, mounted to the front of the smokebox, as opposed to the perhaps more normal practice of having a round door concentric with the circumference of the boiler. He spat on three fingers of his right hand and pressed them to the door. "Damn!" he exclaimed with a confused look. "That's actually hot!"

"Look at those nuts," said Mike. Sure enough, Henry confirmed that some of the many nuts that held the smokebox door closed had been recently manhandled by a wrench, probably one of the wrong size that left marks of bare metal. As Henry jumped off the pilot, Mike ran to the back of the boiler, where the firebox was located, and peered up into the open void where the grate had been removed. The grate held the coal in place while it burned, but allowed the boiler to suck air up into the firebox, through the combustion chamber, and into the flues, facilitating the burning of fuel and the heating of the water in the boiler. Inside the firebox, Mike could see the fire arch and firebrick in place under the crownsheet, and the top of the firebox didn't seem to be so sooty that wind would whip soot up the stack that looked like smoke. "No fire in there."

"Told you." Henry grinned and looked back at the stack. Both men could see that the smoke was getting thicker, though it really didn't look like locomotive smoke.

"Get a wrench," Mike ordered. "I'm going to get to the bottom of this."

While Henry ran into the tool shed, Mike stood on the ground and watched the strange smoke. A few times during his wait, the wind whipped some of it in his direction. It didn't smell like locomotive smoke any more than it looked like it. Instead, Mike decided, it smelled more like burning oil-soaked cotton, like in an old journal box when it gets too hot—but something else he couldn't place.

Just then, Mike saw Todd Lundy, the NNMRR's chief mechanical officer, burst from the side door of the engine shed and slam the storm door hard enough to rattle the loose glass in the shed's hundred-year-old windows. Lundy came marching Mike's way with a giant engine wrench in his left hand, and he looked angry. The mechanic could be imposing even when he wasn't angry, all two hundred fifty pounds of him. Mike could see his cheeks getting ruddier on his chubby face, so chubby at times that it looked like his eyes were being swallowed in the rest of it. His angry squint did nothing to discourage that impression. The hostler ran out of the shed after Lundy, running then to catch up. Henry's eyes were pleading with Mike to calm the angry mechanic.

As if he'd planned to come nose to nose with the general manager and discovered that wasn't going to work, Lundy instead stopped short with the brass buttons on the bib of his overalls about ready to touch Mike Ortega's nose. He addressed curly hair on the top of Mike's head. "Dammit, Mike. You know the operating men aren't supposed to start up doing repairs, even small ones. We have to have some kind of respect for the trades."

This had been an ongoing situation. Lundy had come off a big railroad, where the various crafts and shops, and their respective unions, had always maintained strict separation of duties. A tourist operation like NNMRR saw the whole question of trades and crafts differently, in fact preferring that all employees be familiar with as many tasks as possible. Flexibility and versatility were keys. Wanting to defuse the situation as tactfully as possible, Mike looked up into Lundy's squint and pointed at the front of the locomotive. "Did you or one of your boys do that?"

Lundy's eye followed Mike's arm and finger up to where the nuts had obvious marks on them. "Huh? Hell!" said Lundy as he shifted his weight up and onto the pilot deck. He put a wrench on the nut that was easiest to reach and turned. It swung around without effort, and Lundy gave Mike a confused look while Henry stood by and waited patiently for the apology he thought he had coming. "We don't ever leave these loose like this."

Now Mike swung up onto the pilot. "Let's open her up and see what we've got."

Lundy started grabbing the nuts with both his right and left hand and found that they turned easily. Mike did the same, both of them taking about two minutes to undo all twenty nuts. Lundy pulled a pair of leather work gloves from a back pocket and stuck all eight fingers of both hands behind the door to lug it open. It moved with a groan that echoed through the empty boiler. A billow of thick, grey smoke followed the door and continued to emanate from the now open smokebox. "Damn freaking kids," Lundy said as he stuck his head into the smoke and gloom inside and tried to see what was going on. Then he yelled, "Looks like they threw a bunch of old rags in here and set them on fire, or they spontaneous combusted."

"You want an extinguisher?" Henry yelled from the ground.

Lundy's response was unexpected. "Shit look at this! Goddamn!" He pulled out his head, shaking off the smoke, and said, "I didn't need to see that this morning."

"What?" Mike shoved his own head into the opening. As the smoke from the smoldering rags was starting to clear, he thought that all he was looking at were more rags on the bottom of the smokebox. The bunch of smoking fabric sat crumpled into the space between the nozzle and the feedwater piping on one side. Then his eyes adjusted, and he saw the dead man, partially burned and quite ripe looking, in a smoldering dark blue business suit.

Pulling his head out as fast as he could, and trying to keep from retching, Mike yelled to Henry, "Call the sheriff!"

CHAPTER TWO

(SOMEWHERE SOUTH OF AGUA ROJO, NEW MEXICO, OCTOBER 7, 7:50 A.M.)

On the road again, in yet another rented car, private detective Charlie Komensky and his fiancée, Linda Chelwood, rode without speaking, eyes straight ahead or looking out the side window, never looking at each other, and, certainly, never letting their eyes meet. This wasn't new territory for Charlie, but had rather become a more familiar routine since their impromptu engagement after the Flatwood-Sharedream murders— ridiculously known as *The Flat Tire Murders**--some sixteen months ago.

*The account of Charlie's investigation of the murders of Danny Flatwood and Seth Sharedream is told in *The Flat Tire Murders* available from Pagination Books as an eBook from Amazon for Kindle, as a paperback from CreateSpace, or from the author.

Charlie had never had any problem with the ladies, with the one exception of the only lady he wanted, and she was sitting right next to him. He felt like she was more out of reach than if she were in New Zealand. Charlie sometimes reasoned it out by thinking that, because short, casual relationships with women had come so easy for him in the past, the fair sex had never trained him physically or psychologically for a relationship in which he actually cared for the other women. In his late 40s, but physically fit from a regimen of hard work, running, and occasional training sessions at the police gym, Charlie was the prototype of what women his age wanted. His five-five stature and handsome, Bohemian features—dark hair, dark eyes and eyebrows, and a winning smile—didn't hurt, nor did his owning his own detective agency and handling cases where women seemed to try to use sex to cover up their crimes and misdemeanors.

Linda sniffed a couple of times. The kind of sniff that said to Charlie that it wasn't a cold or an allergy, but that she still wanted him to know she was there even if she didn't want to speak to him. To hear Charlie tell it, he couldn't have done better in a woman, and Linda knew it and reminded him about it regularly; but particularly when the developing tensions between them got to that trigger point. He looked over at her, and she avoided his glance by squinting and looking straight ahead through the bug splattered, dirty windshield. Today her hair was what Charlie had learned in his youth to call dishwater blonde. He never knew why, as most dishwater he had seen looked bluish gray. Linda's long hair, today pulled back in a ponytail, had been straight blonde, brown, and red during the course of their on-again, off-again relationship. He liked the ponytail, but he also liked the long-haired Linda in an evening gown and heels, her face—now devoid of any obvious makeup—looking as runway ready as any model's, or movie starlet's. Linda had been much more successful than Charlie, over the years, in keeping her girlish figure. Slim, and just a hair taller than Charlie, she weighed in at one thirty and counted in at six years his junior. Another reason for Charlie to savor his good luck, though he'd never had trouble establishing short relationships of the casual variety with younger women.

Linda had an ex-husband somewhere, a fact that Charlie usually ignored even in emotionally charged situations. But he wondered if, by putting all of the responsibility to commit on him, she just may have been excusing some of her own reluctance.

Ten miles back on the road from Santa Fe, New Mexico, he'd tried unsuccessfully to lighten the mood by addressing the touchy subject that Linda had been hinting about for at least twelve of the last sixteen months. "Why don't we take this time to talk about setting a date," he proposed as innocently as possible.

A short burst of pyrotechnics followed. "Now? NOW?" she cried. "Do you REALLY want to discuss this now? Now that you've dragged me half way across Great American Southwest HELL, and you've given no thought to anything but TRAINS for the WHOLE TRIP?" She had propped her left leg up on the side of the rented Chrysler 300's console so that her blue-jeaned leg assisted by her left arm propped up with her left hand to the side of her head formed all the barrier she could between her and Charlie, and against any further discussion. He may as well have been looking at a brick wall as at jeans and a white tank top when he looked over at her. That had been the last word until they reached the Pueblo Store in Espanola, where they were able to get out of the car and take a welcome break from each other.

While there, Charlie had realized that his typical driving attire, consisting of blue Dockers, a light cotton sport shirt, and black oxfords that he'd picked off a rack at K Mart, didn't exactly spell "tourist" to the locals, but it didn't exactly say he wasn't from somewhere else. Most of the men there in the travel center—some were Native American and some weren't—wore blue jeans, western shirts, bolo ties with a lot of turquoise, and boots or work shoes. Some wore cowboy hats or summer straws. Charlie wasn't the kind to feel out of place, but he had been spooked by Linda's mood, and he had allowed it to annoy him when most of the aforementioned men had been quite interested in Linda's tight-jeaned, sexy hot, non-local appearance.

In fact, Charlie's old wound from the Flat Tire incident had left him with a noticeable limp that more than once had made him feel more like Linda's father than her lover and fiance. He still wasn't going to budge on getting the extra physical therapy or another operation, no matter how many times she called him stubborn. But the cowboy atmosphere in Espanola, that she seemed to fit right into, gave him pause.

Perhaps it was his fault that not much of the past sixteen months had gone well. Having your girlfriend support you was never a great idea, and seldom a good one. He had spent so much time in physical therapy during those first four months that his private eye business almost shut down, and Linda's savings and profits from her card shop in Oak Brook had gone to pay more than one month's rent on Charlie's office suite. Linda had argued again and again that the rent the suite in Oak Brook was too high, and he'd argued just as often that he needed a high-profile office to get high-profile cases. After that, he struggled to get his salvage business back on a keel even enough to stay a little in the black. Then, on his first case after the therapy, he had been outrun by a suspect five years older than him. Five years! How depressing that had been!

With hurt pride and his usual male testosterone-driven tendency to try and work everything out by himself without letting Linda in on what he was doing, he'd managed to screw things up even worse by Christmas. From Linda's point of view, her man had had no trouble getting on and off trains and locomotives, with their steep and narrow steps and ladders, during his down time. And Charlie didn't really understand why he felt better only when he was out watching or riding trains and not when he was on the job, even though none of the jobs he'd taken had been any more physically demanding. His Christmas gift to her had been this so-called rail cruise that they were on now, and that had been the first time Linda blew up like today; and she hadn't spoken to him for a week.

He'd taken a case involving the theft of something called "quaternaries", which he recalled were some kind of chemicals that made dirty water look cleaner, and found out soon after that the case would take him out of town on New Year's Eve. After exposing a cover-up somewhat more complicated than he'd expected, and seeing that another murderer was put behind bars, he'd at least gotten a good payday with enough money to pay Linda back and then some. But he hadn't gotten back into his office until almost the end of January, and then they'd argued about how much money he was going to pay back. She hadn't wanted any, which he saw as a martyr's position, and he'd wanted to pay it all back at once, which he saw as the only way to get over the feeling that he always owed her something.

Things had seemed to Charlie to have gone on okay after that, but, as it turned out, only to Charlie. Over the Independence Day holiday—he didn't know why he always picked holidays to screw up—Charlie had decided it would be a good time to schedule the rail cruise, before the summer was over and all the good locomotives were locked up in the sheds for the winter. Linda reacted as he should have expected, with certainty and clarity. She presented the facts, in several alternate versions of varying four-letter word content, all of which amounted to the same thing: Linda had been stewing for over a year about setting a date. The harangue reminded him of a Mark Twain monologue telling how a woman, once being started on a course of explaining something she really didn't want to explain, couldn't abide the lid back on the kettle until all the steam had gone.

He knew he was in for another, because the "cruise" had gone no better than the rest of the year, which is to say he was shooting at least 20 over handicap. For a Christmas present, which it was, and a legendary rekindling of their romance, which Charlie had silently hoped it would be, it should have gone spectacularly. But Charlie, being Charlie, had insisted beyond reason that they take a commuter train into Union Station, Chicago, rather than taking a cab or picking a more accessible stop along the route of the Empire Builder. His planning hadn't included the pretty obvious fact that, to catch a 2:15 p.m. train, they'd have to take a middle-of-the-day, milk run that made every stop and really had no place for their baggage. And Linda could not have been persuaded to pack light if she'd been promised a new wardrobe at the other end of the line.

This had started a cascade of other problems; almost more problems than Charlie, driving along the mountain road to Agua Rojo, New Mexico, could remember. A sleeping car had broken down, not affecting them per se, but giving Linda the ammunition to spend the entire first night on the "Builder" fretting about the family of four that had gotten bumped to coach. (Charlie had decided his leg couldn't make a night in coach, but the sleeper hadn't been much better for it.) The train had dragged through one slow order piece of track after another, so that its arrival time in Seattle had been after ten at night instead of half past ten in the morning. They had lost a day of sightseeing as well as their hotel reservations for that night. The resulting "consolation" accommodations, provided by the railroad, had been a disappointment; so, instead of making love, they had wound up watching a bad cable movie and passing out too full of the contents of their mini-fridge.

The trip down the coast later that week had been fantastic, however, and everything had been working smoothly. Charlie felt Linda relax, and he'd felt better, too. A week of sightseeing in the L.A. area followed, including everything from studio tours to a trip up Mulholland Drive, during which Charlie and Linda made out like teenagers. But the romantic part of the trip ended when they had boarded the Southwest Chief to head to Albuquerque. The dining car had been out of service from the get-go, and neither Charlie nor Linda liked microwave food. They'd missed supper, breakfast, and lunch by the time the train had limped into Albuquerque—hours late—towed by an extra locomotive, after one of theirs had shut down somewhere around Winslow, Arizona.

Albuquerque, from the little Charlie had seen of it before they'd gotten a rental and hit the road, seemed like a nice town but a foreign one to an ex-cop from Chicago who had spent most of his police career running and chasing bad guys around the western suburbs thereof. He supposed that there could be enough PI business in a desert community to interest a private dick with his experience, and he had wondered aloud while they waited for the rental agreement to be printed whether Linda would ever like to move to the desert. Her reaction had been, "You just don't ever do anything but beat around the bush. Do you, Komensky?"

"What?" His musing had been innocent.

"When we finish paying for this death march to railroad hell, we won't have enough money left to move to a homeless shelter!"

Now, on the mountain road, she spoke to him for the first time since putting up the Great Left Arm Wall of China. "We better get there soon, or we'll miss the train."

Charlie thought this bode well and checked the GPS map, a concession he made to technology only because it came with the car. "Should be about a mile or two, not long," he concluded. Not more than two minutes later, they passed the sign that said:

AGUA ROJO

POP. 384

ELEV. 7138

Just past the sign, Charlie noticed the narrow gauge railroad tracks running though the bushes along the east side of the roadway. His railfan DNA kicked in and he started looking ahead for plumes of smoke and listening for steam locomotive sounds. In fact, all of his senses were now tuned to railroading, and he immediately forgot the tension between them. Before another minute passed, they were pulling into the crowded "visitor" parking at the NNMRR.

Beyond the beige, clapboard station, Charlie could see that two steam locomotives had been fired up for the day's schedule, and each seemed to be sitting by herself, steaming with the usual hissing, whirring, and thumping of a standing steam locomotive. Neither appeared to be coupled up to a train of any sort. It was then that he noticed that more of the crowd of visitors were hovering around a third, cold locomotive than were taking in the sights of the others; something that didn't seem right to a railfan. Then he noticed the two police cruisers marked for Taos County parked near the two-stall engine house. Before Linda could say anything, he drove up the aisle and stopped the Chrysler behind one of them, and got out. Linda's jaw just worked up and down in silent rage that Charlie would leave her sitting alone in a vehicle illegally parked behind a police car in a strange town in a much stranger county. She had half a mind to get out, walk to the nearest Dairy Queen, and leave the rental there, running, until somebody got in and stole it.

About half way through shouldering his way into the crowd, Charlie encountered a tall man dressed in an old-fashioned conductor's outfit. "How long before the train?" he asked.

"Don't think there's gonna be one," came the terse reply. "Sheriff's gonna make this a crime scene."

"Crime scene? Did somebody steal some parts?"

The conductor just pointed through an opening that had formed in the wall of people. The sheriff had started to shag away some of the gawkers, and Charlie could see what appeared to be a well-dressed but soot-covered man on his back in front of the stationary locomotive. Charlie's first thought was that somebody had been run over by a train, but that was ridiculous. Nothing was moving. As he fought his way closer against the wave of people moving away, Charlie saw that the man's right side appeared charcoaled, perhaps burned, as did the right side of his face. One Taos County deputy stood over the body, taking photos with what looked like a cheap digital camera, and another stood near the cowcatcher of No. 4 with a clipboard and white legal pad on which he was taking notes. The third deputy, a woman, had been trying to shag the crowd, but some kept stopping and turning around. No effort had apparently been made by any of the three to establish a perimeter or protect the deceased from photography.

Charlie couldn't help himself. "Who's in charge here?" he asked while ignoring the female deputy's raised palm. He had directed the question at the two guys by the body, but she answered him nonetheless. "Taos County Sheriff. Please move along."

"I'm a private detective from Chicago, and I'd like to offer my assistance."

As he reached for his wallet in his back pocket, he saw the deputy—Bernice Shrader, her name pin said—put her hand on her holstered gun, ready to react. He could see it was a Glock 7. New Mexicans were serious about their firearms, as he had learned by seeing the many visitors to the pueblo travel center who carried openly, so he took it slow and easy. Bernice was shorter than the male deputies, and, though he had no doubt she was physically fit under her ill-fitting uniform, she struck Charlie as being "squishy." Her dirty blonde hair had been pulled up to be concealed under her Smoky Bear hat. Charlie made a mental note that most of the law enforcement he had seen so far in New Mexico appeared to be wearing uniforms designed in the 1940s. He handed her his wallet and let her open it herself. "How do you pronounce that last name?" She looked up at him and squinted.

"What the winter resorts up here want people to do. 'Come 'n' ski,'" he answered, giving her his best, broad grin.

"Fine then, Charles Come and Ski," she said, smiling back. "I guess we could use some advice, seeing as none of us has ever had a murder on our plate before this."

"What makes you think it's murder?" he asked, interest piqued.

The deputy started rattling off facts like a typewriter. "The deceased was found inside that locomotive at about seven this morning. Somebody had set fire to oily rags stuffed into the locomotive, and that's what alerted the manager of the railroad to check inside. They pulled the deceased down there, hoping there was some life left in him, but our best guess is that the death occurred before the fire was set."

"You're missing something."

"Enlighten us." The other two deputies had started listening in on their conversation.

"Have you thought of suicide?"

One of the tall deputies spoke up this time. "Mister, those twelve nuts that hold the front door shut were hand tightened. This man didn't do that from inside the boiler."

"Have you talked to everyone who could have put the nuts back on? Say, because they found them off and were just covering for a friend's mistake?"

"Not yet," said the third deputy. Both of the two men were young, clean-shaven, non-Hispanics. Contrary to Bernice's appearance, they both looked like they took hours every morning to get their uniforms just right. The spit polish on their shoes hadn't been dimmed by walking around in the sandy ballast of the house track, and their hats—worn at the prescribed angle—wouldn't have blown off in a high wind.

Charlie looked back at the Chrysler, in which Linda was lounging, a picture of pure displeasure. Her angry eyes met his immediately, and he took the coward's way out and looked back at the three deputies. They seemed to be waiting for Charlie to offer up another suggestion, and he had plenty of them.

He was about to suggest that they clear a perimeter that included the locomotive, engine shed, and any tools that could have been used to remove and re-apply the nuts, when another voice came from behind him. "See, that's the problem. I've got a railroad to run." The voice came from Mike Ortega, who was talking to somebody on Bluetooth.

Almost without thinking first, Charlie swung around to face Ortega. "You run this place?" he asked, interrupting Ortega's conversation.

Ortega looked at him and said to his call, "Just a second." Then he took his hand down from the device. "Who are you?"

"I just happen to be a big fan of steam locomotives." Ortega started almost instantly to return to his call, so Charlie added, "But I also just happen to be a private detective and an expert in murder investigations."

This caught Ortega's attention, and he told the caller he'd call back. Extending a hand, he stated, "I'm Mike Ortega, general manager." Then he asked, "So who called you?"

"Nobody, I'm on vacation with my extremely bored fiancée." He nodded toward Linda. "But it appears that you may be in need of the services of a detective who's an expert in both your field and mine."

Charlie knew that a general axiom in the railroad industry was that a railfan, derogatorily known as a "foamer," especially one who claimed to be railroad savvy, probably didn't know anything about real railroading and probably couldn't be trusted to stay safely on the property without killing himself or somebody else. So Charlie had taken a big chance espousing an expertise in railroading. But he had an ace in the hole; and that was his longtime friend Judge Elmo Burmeister. Burmeister had stepped down from the bench in the time since Charlie's wound had become an issue, but he had hooked Charlie up over the years with several cases involving lost freight, stolen equipment, or passenger liability; and Burmeister, a railfan himself, had represented several railroads in Illinois before being put on the bench. The only thing that could go wrong was really that he hadn't warned the judge that he would be using him for a reference to snag some railroad-related detective work.

Charlie recognized that he had surprised Ortega when the latter hesitated and looked around him as though he were thinking that he didn't need another crazy twist to his already messed up day, so he said, "Don't have to decide this moment. Just think about the fact that I can see . . . oh, maybe ten things going on within ten feet of the dear departed that shouldn't be." He looked around as if looking for more. Really, he was just hoping to actually see ten, but he said, "And that's just for starters."

Ortega shrugged, but Charlie couldn't tell if it was an "I don't care" shrug or an "I give up" one. "Look, I don't know you from Adam, and I've got a board of directors to answer to, so you can participate if you want to risk your own dollar and neck, as far as I'm concerned."

"Great!" Charlie turned to Deputy Schrader, but he immediately felt a hand on his shoulder. It was Ortega.

"You didn't let me finish," said Ortega gruffly. "You have to sign the standard liability waiver first."

As they walked to the small office that the railroad had rented in a storefront across the street, Charlie held up his hand to let Linda know he was signaling her that it would just take five more minutes. He then realized how cold his hand was; numbing cold. The morning temperature at the high elevation couldn't have been more than 55, and he knew that Linda would be freezing if he hadn't left the Chrysler running with the heat on. Stranded without warm clothing would be yet another thing that would give her motive to kill him and leave his body in a nearby canyon. The thought made him feel that much colder.

The front of the building where Ortega took him had been remodeled with faux wood siding so that the office of the railroad was right inside the half-glass front door where the original store space had been. The small office had a space heater going near the back door, but it was still cold. Instead of plaster, the walls were finished in beaded millwork and painted light green, like the inside of a 19th century railroad station. Ortega's roll-top desk echoed the theme, as did a number of wall-hung posters of train schedules and passenger trains of the past, and a loudly-ticking Regulator station clock. Charlie hoped that he wouldn't have to sign the release with a quill pen, but the afforded ballpoint worked well enough.

Before Charlie could dot the i on his first name—he always used Charlie and not Charles—both men heard a loud rapping on the glass of the front door. Charlie looked up to see probably a baker's dozen angry tourist railfans demanding entry. "When's the train ride gonna start?" yelled one of them, and as he did so, Charlie could see a few more people running over from across the street.

"Wasn't a good idea to let the crowd see us walk over here," observed Charlie. "Somebody in the crowd knows where you live."

Ortega looked a little surprised, or at least like a fish out of water, and he abruptly ordered Charlie, "You handle it?"

"Can we talk money?"

"Okay! Okay! I'll pay your standard fee if you get this whole mess organized and get us back on the rails."

Charlie didn't need another cue. He stepped to the front door, threw it open, and yelled, "No train today. Spread the word! No train today!"

A voice from the back angrily yelled, "Who says!"

"I'm a railroad detective, and I say." Then he bluffed, "If you've never been arrested by a railroad cop, you'll get your chance if you don't get off the property in five minutes." The closest member of the group, the one right up into the doorway, looked incredulous. "Well? What are you waiting for?" Charlie hoped that his threat would be taken seriously, and it was. Several men split off from the back of the crowd and were clearly okay with spreading the word. In a few seconds, only the incredulous one in the door remained, and it remained only for Charlie to scowl at him and lunge a bit in his direction to get him to move.

When Charlie turned back to Ortega, the latter had his head in his hands. "What are you doing?" he said through his palms. "You just turned away a whole day's customers."

"Seriously? Do you think you're going to have any trains running after the Sheriff Andy 'aw shucks' Taylor crowd over there get through fucking this up? What we want is for the coroner—or whoever you got here in the mountains that serves as one—to come in here and be absolutely certain that he doesn't want to call in any more help and tie up your railroad for a week. My way, you should be back on the rails by tomorrow morning."

(NORTHERN NEW MEXICO RAILROAD, AGUA ROJO, NM, OCTOBER 7, LATE MORNING)

It had taken Charlie and Mike Ortega another twenty minutes to set the ground rules of his involvement and put in place a handshake agreement for Charlie to get paid if he got results. The railroad man also related the story of how and where they had found the body that morning. When Charlie stepped from the front door of the little storefront, he did so just in time to see Linda lugging her suitcase to a small motel down the street. On reaching his rental car, he found her message to him in the form of her having left all four doors of the vehicle open with the engine running and the trunk open. "Why didn't she just tell me she's not happy," he said to himself with his usual reluctance to accept that she really always communicated with him through these not-so-subtle hints.

The crowd had mostly disbursed, as evidenced by the sudden availability of parking spaces; although a few diehards still hovered near the two hot steam locomotives. Charlie discovered, without too much further ado, that the three deputies had managed to keep everyone off the cold engine, where the body had been found, and out of an area that would have been the likely place for there to be any immediate evidence of who did the bad deed. Because the deputies were still reluctant to cooperate with Charlie's pushy, Chicago ways, he enlisted four of the engine shop crew to establish a wider perimeter that included the engine shed and shop. He didn't think that including the station would do any good, as that ship had sailed as soon as the first customer had strolled in for a ticket that morning. One of the shop crew found some red crepe paper from the previous Fourth of July, and that had to do for crime scene tape until somebody came up with something better. The question, "You seriously don't carry it?" had been followed by blank stares from the deputies.

Just about forty minutes after his talk with Ortega, a white car showed up with a State of New Mexico seal on the side and lettering that simply said:

OMI

"Oh, my! Who's OMI?" Charlie asked one of the deputies, pronouncing the initials as "oh, my" to make a point.

"Office of the Medical Investigator. I guess coroner to you. This one's a deputy from the funeral home in Taos. Sam Speeno."

The Medical Investigator had gotten out of his car and started walking toward the group that included the three deputies and Charlie. Speeno had a pronounced limp, a bit worse than Charlie's, and carried a walking stick carved out of a tree limb. He wore a plaid, flannel, mid-length coat over his sturdy, well-fed torso, and a pair of little used hiking shoes. His face was birdlike with a very pointy nose, wire-rimmed glasses, and thick, gray eyebrows, topped by a Tyrolean hat with a bird feather that seemed out of place in New Mexico. Charlie walked to meet the Medical Investigator halfway. On the way, he noted that the man's beard resembled a badly trimmed version of Colonel Sanders.

"Are you somebody I'm supposed to talk to?" The question surprised Charlie, partly because he didn't know the answer, and partly because the man's Northern New Mexico accent was so unexpected.

"I'm Charlie Komensky," he answered, offering his hand. "I guess you could say I'm a railroad detective."

"I did not get your name. Charlie Ko Men?"

"Komensky."

"Could you please spell that for me."

Charlie did.

"Charlie Mensky," said Speeno, proud of his pronunciation even though it was wrong. "And you are the detective for the railroad?"

"Yes, for this murder investigation."

Speeno pulled his head back on his neck and pushed his chin down into the front of his coat, actually onto the large turquoise and silver slide of a bolo tie he was wearing. "Who says murder? Do you?"

"We were hoping you could tell us." Charlie gestured in the direction of the three deputies.

"I don't know if I'm even supposed to be speaking to you. So if you will please excuse me." Speeno walked away without shaking Charlie's hand, and Charlie followed to the spot where the body still rested. When Speeno noticed, he said to Deputy Schrader, "Out of respect for the dead, I'm thinking that it would be good for you all to give me some privacy as I poke and prod at this poor gentleman. Could you do that?"

All three deputies seemed to look to Charlie for it to be okay to do that. "Okay, I can respect that," was Charlie's answer, and they all walked closer to the entrance to the shop. It bothered Charlie that there seemed to be nothing he could do to move matters in a forward direction, and he was equally frustrated by the apparent lack of urgency in all the other participants save Mike Ortega. And he had to ask himself how much expertise a funeral director could bring to the Office of Medical Investigator.

He needed to do . . . something! "Bernice? Can I call you Bernice? Your department doesn't have a CSU?" She shook her head. "Do we know that State Police have one on the way?"

"ETA is 35 minutes."

As he thought about other things to do, Charlie kept his eyes on Speeno. The man was a queer one, to say the least. Speeno started by engaging in what looked like a ritual circling of the body, which still rested on its back in the middle of the two rails in front of the locomotive pilot where, presumably, Mike Ortega and his hostler had placed it after removing it from the smokebox. During the first revolution, Speeno used his carved walking stick in the usual manner, partly for swagger and partly to support his right-leg limp. On the second revolution, be began a larger circle and started pointing the business end of the stick at the body, first at the head, then at the shoulder, eventually making another complete circle. To Charlie, this seemed very odd, indeed.

The next circle, Speeno started to pause here and there, pushing the end of the walking stick at, and into places on the corpse: under the armpits, beneath the lapels of the expensive suit jacket, under the buttocks, behind the neck. Charlie was just about to go over and object to the weird way that Speeno was treating the situation when he realized that Speeno was talking to himself, as well. Then Charlie spotted the small earpiece in Speeno's left ear, and realized that he also had a small video viewfinder projecting down from under the brim of the Tyrolean hat. "Damn!" said Charlie to himself. "The old fart has some high tech in that stick and is recording a first examination, and taking videos to boot!" He suddenly had new respect for this apparent eccentric from the Taos funeral parlor.

After another thirty seconds, Charlie couldn't control himself. Leaving the deputies still wondering what to do next, he excitedly strode over to Speeno. When he got within ten feet of Speeno's back, the medical investigator held up a hand like a traffic cop, and Charlie stopped in his tracks. "If you are not going to stand your ground," said Speeno without taking his attention from the stick, "you can go get some gloves and help me turn this poor man over onto his side so I can see what's underneath him." Speeno apparently didn't see any reason to explain his unorthodox poking and prodding, or assumed that Charlie had already figured it out. Either way, Charlie readily complied and begged some latex from Deputy Schrader. One of the male deputies cracked a crude joke about whether she always provided latex on the first date, and she didn't even flinch.

As Charlie approached Speeno and the deceased this time, Speeno stood back and bobbed his head up and down in an exaggerated way that Charlie took as a signal he was ready for Charlie to get in position. Charlie got down in a squat and got one hand under the corpse's left shoulder and the other under the left buttock. When he looked up, he found that Speeno was no longer on the other side of the body, but rather had climbed up on the locomotive pilot and was now leaning into the smokebox taking pictures with his crazy walking stick.

Charlie took the opportunity to examine the body. This was the closest he had been, and it wasn't pretty. The smell of burning and dead flesh hit him in the face like an ugly fist. The side of the body he was holding appeared relatively undamaged, with a good coating of soot. The torn left arm of the suit jacket, he supposed, was where the corpse had been dragged out of the locomotive. The victim—now that he was touching the body, it became more real that this was a formerly living person that had suffered a death—appeared to be in his early 40s, although bloating may have already been concealing facial wrinkles that would say he was older. He was well trimmed and had probably shaved with a straight razor or very good electric razor within hours of being killed. A medium skinned Caucasian, he appeared to Charlie to be of southern European or Mediterranean heritage.

The man was bald with a fringe of black hair, and Charlie looked over the top of the head and found no marks or indications of a blow or a struggle. No blood from the ears, and, rocking the vic up from the track, Charlie could see no evidence of blood or trauma in the hair above the neck. So much for the left side of the body. The right side was different. That was the side where the rag fire had done the most damage. Although Charlie could see that the vic had probably been good looking, with a straight, almost Roman nose and good teeth, the right side of the face had been burned to the extent that there was charcoal and tissue destruction well into the musculature and bone of the face and forehead. The contraction from the muscles on the burned side had drawn the vic's lips into a sneer, unless that was the way he always was. "Good motive for murder," Charlie told himself.

Below the face, the jacket had done a reasonable job of protecting the body, with the exception of where the right kneecap had been burned to the bone, revealing a prosthetic joint. Charlie concluded that the vic had been positioned in a fetal position on his right side or with his right side to the fire, so the face and knees were both close to the hottest part. The murderer, for this was most certainly murder in Charlie's book, had perhaps not wanted the facial features to be identified, and set the fire to cover it up. What had Ortega told him about the fire? Rags ignited by what? Charlie knew they would look for a matchbook or a discarded lighter, but yet somehow that they wouldn't find one or the other. All these things ran through Charlie's detective sieve and sifted out for later consideration.

"Would you give thought to lifting him again for me?" Charlie jumped a little when he heard and found that Speeno was standing right over him, then dutifully lifted the body so that the unburned side was exposed to Speeno's probing walking stick.

After a minute or two, during which Charlie's arms became fatigued, and the stooping made his bad leg hurt, he cried out, "Need a break here!"

"Just one more second and I am completed."

Charlie let the vic roll back and gingerly pulled his gloved hands out from underneath. After he stood up, he addressed Speeno, who hadn't moved but stood looking over the body with his stick held easily in his right hand much as if he were on a scenic viewpoint on a high cliff. "Nice piece of tech you got there."

Speeno sniffed, then looked at the end of the stick where Charlie could see a small camera lens that looked like a miniature of a sighting scope from a sniper's rifle. "When you have arthritis and lumbago, you use whatever methods are suitable to keep from bending and stooping." Then he changed the subject, and said, "I would very much like to spend the day chit-chatting, but I would prefer that we stick to the business of solving this murder."

"Then you now agree that this is a homicide?"

Looking at Charlie's face, Speeno observed, "You are overjoyed?"

"Just a little happy to have suspicions confirmed."

"What else would you like me to confirm?" Speeno tapped his stick on the side of Charlie's leg, sending up a momentary lance of pain that made Charlie wince. "Oh, I'm sorry. It seems that you, too, are somewhat hobbled."

"You're too observant not to have seen that," Charlie said angrily.

"Then we understand each other." Speeno touched his earpiece as if he were receiving a call, but said to Charlie, "Again I ask, what would you like me to confirm?"

"Time of death?"

"From lividity, the heat from the fire, rigor and other factors, I'd say before midnight last night, but no earlier than nine. I'll do more tests."

"You have a thermometer in that stick, too?" Charlie was sorry he asked as soon as he said it.

"Yes, and also a pointy tip to poke into the ribs of annoying detectives. Did you think that, because you are an educated man from Chicago with quite a reputation that I was just a bumpkin from the mountains who came down to the flats only for fishing and to, as you Anglos say, tie one on?"

"How did you . . . ?" Charlie stopped when he realized that Speeno was getting a constant stream of information both from the small video screen and through the earpiece.

Speeno saw Charlie's consternation and, for the first time, smiled broadly. "Charles Komensky, I am Samuel Marcus Speeno, at your service."

At that, Charlie relaxed a little and stowed for future use the apology his brain had been brewing. "I guess I'll have to assume that you know everything about me."

The MI didn't address the statement, but instead said, "I, unlike yourself, was initially reluctant to play the murder card, but then was dealt a hand in spades when I lifted the left breast of that fine cotton blend jacket he is wearing."

Charlie bent over and lifted the jacket fabric with one hand. Almost perfectly centered on the victim's left breast, a round had penetrated his shirt, leaving little or no blood. Charlie's mind went through the possible arms that could have caused this hole, and while doing so, it was not lost on him that there had been no bleeding. "This man was shot after his heart had stopped beating, and either the jacket was wide open or he was not wearing it when shot. Somebody killed him, then shot him—with maybe a .40 Smith and Wesson or an old Nevada Standard, and then put his jacket on." Speeno nodded his agreement. "Were there any . . . ?"

"No," interrupted the MI. "Not a trace of a gunshot having been fired inside or into the locomotive boiler."

"But the tears on his sleeve suggest that the body was dumped up there after the jacket was on the body."

"Precisely." Speeno then seemed to be thinking again, took a step toward the locomotive, and then said, "If the body had been more burned, we could have seen this as a gunshot victim instead of . . . well, something else."

"What else?"

"Chemical or biological. We'll just have to see. Maybe somebody poisoned their lawyer."

It took a while for Speeno's quip to sink in. "Lawyer?" Speeno was smiling ever so slightly, and Charlie's words came out not just a little annoyed. "Why didn't you tell me you know who he is, or was?"

"Not only do I know who he was, but I knew him."

Charlie waited for an explanation, or a name, but it didn't come. As soon as the silence from Speeno became uncomfortable for Charlie, he asked, "Don't you think you should recuse yourself, or something? You know the victim. You can't possibly be objective."

"Oh, not like that." Speeno stretched out the word "that" to emphasize that it wasn't an intimate knowledge. "I knew him more by . . . by reputation. I am just a little bit of a student of the American judiciary, and I have read extensively with regards to a case this gentleman was involved in—I want to say in California—about three years ago."

Although he wanted to ask for a name, Charlie went where the story was going. "Was it a murder case? Or high-profile? Did it involve railroads?"

"Let me see." This time, Speeno stretched the word "let." "Our *hombre muerto* was defending a Vegas mobster who had gotten into a little problem with a *prostitutita* , just a little bit underage, who was found in the Los Angeles River with the mobster's wedding ring clutched in one hand. The *abogado* was very effective."

"I follow, but could we just stick to English?" When the MI just looked at Charlie like he didn't know what he was talking about, Charlie realized that the smattering of Spanish was probably normal for the area. "Do you remember his name?"

"I remember he got the slime off."

"But no name."

"You are fortunate." Speeno held a hand up to the earpiece. "That information is just coming in from the pictures that I emailed to State Police."

"You did all that from . . . ?"

"Shhh! The name is Dinwiddie. First name Eran. Originally from Chicago, had a law partner named Maynot in Chicago, then opened an office in Los Angeles. Retired from the bar just after the little prostitute's murder trial."

Charlie told Speeno he didn't remember the law firm, but it would depend on how far back we were talking. "Some of these wise guys go way, way back, even before my time in Chicago," he observed.

"So that explains your accent," said Speeno, and then he grinned from ear to ear.

He supposed that it would do no good to point out that Speeno's strange way of speaking English sounded just as weird to Charlie and his Chicago brogue sounded to a northern New Mexican, so he decided to focus again on the body. He was just about to say that a good theory would be that the lawyer was poisoned or drugged to death, then shot and dumped into the locomotive to burn in order to throw them off as to the real cause of death. He didn't get a chance, however, because Speeno saw the mobile crime lab pulling up, and he turned away from Charlie.

It didn't bother Charlie, who put his hands in his pockets and walked over to the locomotive. It was a beauty, and Charlie wished he could see it running, or run it himself. It beckoned him to climb on it, or in it, and not for the purposes of investigating a crime. Charlie couldn't control himself, and found himself up on the pilot deck while nobody was looking. The railroad crew seemed to be talking among themselves, probably, thought Charlie, about losing a day's pay. Speeno was still talking to the two techs and the three deputies next to the mobile lab, a souped up version of a recreational vehicle that was painted in gaudy southwestern colors right off of a movie set.

Something ground under Charlie's shoe, and he looked down, imagining it to be a cinder. Instead, he saw the glint of the high-altitude sun off something glittering and sending out rainbow sparks of light, just like something Charlie had seen when he was moonlighting as a jewelry store guard back in the day. He bent over and picked up the stone, a diamond he thought would be pushing two carats. Had this stone come from the pockets of the corpse? Impulsively, he pocketed the diamond and hustled off the pilot before anyone saw him up there. The value of the diamond would be somewhere in the range of seven to ten thousand dollars, but that wasn't why he was keeping it. He had seen evidence with value go astray before, and he didn't trust anyone who lived in this impoverished corner of the country to resist the temptation of keeping the diamond for profit. He believed the aphorism, "Good things come in small packages," but also knew that, "Good things in small packages are easily stolen."

He had also seen good evidence used badly when investigators didn't know what they had and prosecutors, who rely on their investigators, botched the cases. Charlie's experience with gemstones made him think the evidence could be better preserved and followed in his hands. The crime scene unit would probably closely examine the gem, and they would know that laser inscription or identification was a common thing. They wouldn't necessarily know that many cuts also include coded information, like the conceit of a painter leaving a stray brushstroke in his paintings to validate his work. It was perhaps as much a conceit, one that would get him in trouble, that he thought he would know how to follow these leads better than a deputy from a five-man department.

Then, too, he hoped—in some miracle of irrelevance—the gem was just something lost near the railroad eons ago that would never be missed. Finders keepers. It would solve a lot of his financial problems, or make a neat start on a real ring for Linda. So why let it get put into a plastic bag and sit on a shelf for thirty years or until the death-penalty appeals ran out, whichever came first in this state.

Thinking of Linda reminded him that he'd better get going and take control of the investigation to the extent possible, so that his prediction that the authorities would shut down the railroad for a week would not come true. That would be a credibility disaster of epic proportions, especially the way he'd been treating Linda today. As he patted the pocket of his Dockers where he expected that the stone would not be noticed among his keys and his pocket knife, Charlie saw a silver Mercedes G-Class SUV pulling out in front of the motel across the street where Linda had gone to rent a room. It gave him a shiver, not from any premonition or gut hunch, but when he recognized the reminder that Linda really could do so much better. The driver of that high-rent vehicle certainly had to be better off financially than Charlie had ever been. He made a mental note to try to treat her better—when this was all over—never remotely realizing that this was probably the thousandth such mental note he'd made that year.

Oddly enough, when he got himself over to the rest of the group near the "Crime Scene Winebago," he found that Deputy Schrader had been anointed to head the investigation for the—as it turned out, nine-member not five—Taos County Sheriff's Office. Charlie marveled that he should encounter two murder cases in less than two years where the police force with jurisdiction didn't have a professional homicide cop. Not that his own particular expertise had really solved the last one, as it had been more the stupidity of the criminal. Part of him hoped it would be the same here, but he doubted it. Compared to a small businessman murdered in his shop, a mob attorney victim of premeditation seemed more complicated.

In any case, he thought he had hit it off with Deputy Schrader. "Call me Bernie," she said as he started to make suggestions for expediting the investigation. Her smile was genuine and friendly and made her a good home stretch more appealing as a woman than her earlier gun-touching persona had suggested she could be. Feminine or not, he noticed she still liked to lean that hand on the Glock.

Before the sun had passed the zenith, Charlie and Bernie had the real crime-scene tape strung from the locomotive and around the back of the two nearest buildings, and the two male deputies—who still seemed to think they had better things to do on the force than take orders from an aging private eye—were helping one of the CSTs scour the shop and the engine shed for anything of use. In the process, the pair of deputies were supposed to interview the railroad's workers and volunteers for any leads. The other tech helped Bernie go over the outside of the locomotive, and then both techs got into the smokebox and went over the guts of the boiler with a fine tooth comb and digital camera. The process was laborious but fruitful. Though Charlie didn't know what they would lead to, they had more clues by four o'clock: Thread pulled from the smokebox promised to be mostly from the deceased's suit, but could be from other clothing— they'd have to rule out the shopmen's clothes as well as whatever Ortega and Henry, the hostler, were wearing. Despite the burned and oil-soaked rags, the techs pulled a decent footprint from the smokebox—a dress shoe sized eight that had been repaired by a professional shoemaker. And a partial palm print was located on a railhead a scant four inches in front of the pilot, as though perhaps the person who hid the body had leaned on the railhead to steady himself—or herself—after stumbling with the load.

No other gemstones were found, although three inches of cinder ballast from around the front of the locomotive had yielded two wedding rings, a rhinestone engagement ring in a cheap setting, and a handful of Cracker Jack toys and odd pieces of other objects that had been dropped there over the years. One of the wedding rings had the date of the nuptials as June 12, 1956, so God only knew how long it had rested just under the surface of the track bed. As far as the interviews were concerned, Charlie decided they were not up to his standards but would do to get things moving. Without exception, the crewmembers agreed that the locomotive had been dormant for three weeks, which was the last time anyone had worked on it.

When everybody had compared notes, it was decided— by Deputy Schrader with prodding from Charlie—that the scene could be released to the property owner, and any further investigation would not be jeopardized by the railroad running tomorrow. Charlie breathed a sigh of relief at that, feeling that he had now earned any fees Mike Ortega could squeeze out of his board of directors. OMI Speeno was to transport the corpse to the morgue near University Hospital in Albuquerque, and, as usual, no promise was made as to when laboratory and other results would be available. "We don't even have enough live doctors in this state to treat the living, so the dead will wait. They usually don't complain," Speeno quipped. With everything else bagged and tagged and packed up, including the wedding rings, Charlie's thoughts turned to Linda. Now which motel did she go to?

Bernie saw Charlie looking up and down the street across from the railroad yards and guessed what he was thinking. "Are you looking for your friend?" Charlie nodded, but kept looking. "She sure looked pissed off at you! I think she went over to the Cerro Grande down at the end of the block. They got a nice room for the price."

Charlie had his ass back in the rental and out of the lot without saying another word.

CHAPTER THREE

(AGUA ROJO, NEW MEXICO, OCTOBER 7, 4:01 P.M.)

The Cerro Grande looked like a passable motel, as far as Charlie was concerned. None of the usual chain motel logos had caught his attention on the short drive over. He didn't recall any along the last fifty miles of road they'd traveled that morning, either, and he made a mental note to suggest to Mike Ortega that a tourist town needed a Holiday Inn or a Motel 6 or 2—or 10. The Cerro looked like a motel that had been thrown up in the sixties, making it about as old as he was, and he couldn't decide if the architecture was meant to be a combination of California Mission and Swiss Alpine, or if he was looking at an unfamiliar style. Located on a corner lot with large trees behind, a roof of Spanish tiles, and ornamental iron railings, the yellow stucco, two story, L-shaped building was pretty enough until you got in close, and then it showed its age.

He started by pulling up into the entrance between the main office and the outdoor pool. Leaving the motor running, he ran into the office to receive a grand reception from nobody. No bell, no call button, nothing by which he could summon a clerk, owner or manager came to his attention. Guessing that it being mid-afternoon and likely they weren't expecting guests this early—although Linda had been much earlier—he decided to glide the Chrysler into a parking space and wait until somebody went back to the office. After all, how long could it be? Then he drifted off.

When he awoke suddenly and realized his mistake, a tall, white-shirted clerk stood in the office with two customers from a Hyundai SUV now parked where he had started. He looked at his Timex and realized he'd been asleep for an hour, and the clerk hadn't accosted him. Even with the windows open, the high altitude sun had done its best, and it was hot in the car. Hoping he didn't stink of sweat, he went in and patiently waited for the two customers to trundle off to their room.

When he finally got his chance to ask about Linda, the clerk, who had fuzzy, short, red hair and a forehead that pinched together as he moved his eyes, looked at Charlie as if he were an ax murderer. "The woman in that room told me not to give out any information to any men who came asking for her."

Charlie was incredulous. It went beyond any demonstrations she had staged before. Here, in a strange town, that she would set him up to be a perceived stalker or battering boyfriend, knowing him and his temperament as she did? He paused to regain his composure, then walked out into the late afternoon sunlight.

(BENSENVILLE, ILLINOIS, OCTOBER 7, 6:10 P.M. CDT)

The big steam locomotive had just completed a run from the west coast into the yards in Bensenville, Illinois, with a few stops in between. At that exact moment, Charlie Komensky stood outside the Cerro Grande Motel in Agua Rojo, New Mexico, and watched its distant cousin, one of the narrow gauge locomotives of the Northern New Mexico Railroad, back into an engine house stall so its fires could be banked for the night. The group that had just spent almost $1 million dollars and countless hours restoring the bigger locomotive had taken her—despite size, they also referred to the big eight-coupled engine as female—on a shakedown from Milwaukee to Seattle and then to Chicago. After fueling the oil-burning locomotive, they would drive her to a museum in Northern Illinois for a week of cold display during the museum's year-end festivities; then they planned to run her back to Milwaukee for the winter. The insurance costs for the move alone had almost bankrupted the group, known as the Friends of Milwaukee Steam. Only recently had an anonymous benefactor come forward with some hope, and the expectation for the group was to be able to start the new season next spring with all of their insurance costs underwritten.

The steam facilities in the yard had long since given way to a diesel shop, so the volunteer engineer had parked the big engine next to a concrete pad in the area where two sanding towers and a row of eight fuel pumps serviced the diesels. As he pulled down off the cab, following the fireman, the engineer noticed a short, older, bearded man in his sixties talking on a cheap cell phone. Although the man wasn't wearing a hardhat or an ID badge, the engineer wasn't either, so he told himself, "Probably a railfan from one of the local railroad clubs."

The man with the cellphone paid only scant attention to the spectacular locomotive, however, and seemed concerned only with the whereabouts of the person on the other end of the call. "It doesn't matter if he found it. I don't care if that puts you in jeopardy. I just want to know when can you get back here. Okay, do what you think best. No, never mind. I'll have another project for you when you get here, but it's gotta be before the end of next week, so don't schmuck around too long." The short man snapped the cheap phone shut and then walked to the front of the engine to scrutinize the big circular door that covered the front of the smokebox. He made a few mental notes, and then sauntered toward the road that crossed the tracks at the west end of the engine house. None of 1242's group noticed as the short man got into a black, beat up German sedan and drove away.

(AGUA ROJO, NEW MEXICO, 5:15 P.M. MDT)

When Charlie cooled down, he dug in his pocket to see if he had any hard cash. Finding only a twenty and a ten, he looked around to see if there was an ATM on the premises. After running across the street to the Chevron, he again approached the motel clerk. The man tried to only half look at him. Laying a C-note on the counter he also flipped open his wallet with his investigator's ID and his federal court ID. Either was probably meaningless, but he hoped the point wouldn't be lost on the clerk. "Just give me a room number."

The clerk shook his head, but focused his gaze on the hundred.

"How much for both the room number and a key?"

Now the clerk seemed agitated, looking to the right and left to see if anyone was watching or if he were being recorded. "I . . . um."

Charlie started counting banknotes, very slowly. When he got to four, the clerk reached under the desk, quickly coded a key card, and wrote 213 on the front with marker. Charlie took the key card, pulled a hundred from the stack, and said, "You'll get the other hundred if you don't call the sheriff for the next hour." As the clerk reached for the cash, Charlie grabbed his wrist. "Just so you know, she's not the one in danger. If you hear a gunshot, it'll probably be me that needs an ambulance." He winked at the clerk and released his wrist. The man squirreled up his forehead and gave a dirty look and then pretended he needed to tend to anything else but Charlie.

After getting his rolling suitcase from the trunk of the rental, he found 213 to be a room off in the corner of the L-shape and hidden from view from the main street but not from the side road that he had crossed to get to the Chevron. He paused a minute to collect his thoughts. He had no idea how he was going to approach Linda, but knew her well enough to know she had a sense of humor as well as a way of acting out when she didn't like something. How bad could it be? Pretty bad. He noticed she had the drapes pulled. He knocked.

Nothing. No response.

Again. This time harder. Still nothing. Well, here goes!

He pushed in the key card and heard the click as the green light went on.

"If that's you, Charlie Komensky, you better be prepared to grovel." It was Linda's voice from inside the room.

There's a chance! Charlie smiled and opened the door. "Anybody home?"

The wine bottle just missed his head, shattering above the door and splattering the remainder of its red contents onto the back of his jacket. Linda sat at the small, round table that was shoved into the corner opposite the door with another empty in her hand and ready to fling. With the drapes closed, the room appeared drab, and Charlie didn't notice or care much about the decoration, just about Linda. The same outfit she had arrived in that morning looked much more rumpled, and her red eyes and eyelids told him she had been crying. Charlie's expression changed from joviality to concern, and she noticed. "You didn't give a shit all day, so don't try to tell me you care about my feelings now." Charlie ducked and fended off the second throw, knocking the second empty to the bed.

He walked to the foot of the bed but hesitated to go any closer, considering she hadn't yet thrown her purse or the table lamp. "Sweetheart—you know I care about you!" Now that his eyes had adjusted to the only light in the room—coming from the bathroom—he could see that she had a "rocks" glass in her hand with dregs from red wine. He knew she didn't handle red wine well, and made the mistake of saying, "It's the wine talking."

"No. No! Charlie, this is me talking," Linda sobbed. The white tank top had a large wine stain under her right breast.

Charlie nudged closer to the table and gestured to the only other chair. "Mind if I sit?"

"You can go straight to hell!" She threw the empty glass, and he caught it in his right hand and placed it gently on the table.

"Honey, I know the trip has been stressful. But this is business. I . . . " He stopped because she was pointing toward the door, and mental dawn was breaking. "You want me out?" She nodded her assent, still pointing. "I get it. You still need some time alone."

"Alone, Charlie? Alone?" she almost screamed. "That's all I've been is alone. I want you to get out and stay out. I'm going to drink myself to sleep, if I can find another bottle of wine, and I'm taking the rental—which my credit card is paying for—and catching a Southwest flight from Albuquerque tomorrow morning at six. If you come within a mile of trying to stop me, I'll make sure the TSA thinks you eat children. They'll hold you for days." She spat out the last word as if she meant an eternity of days, and all Charlie could do was stand there with his mouth open. He just couldn't comprehend what he'd just heard.

"Are we . . . ?"

"The word is over, Charlie. O - very, very, very, o – ver."

He pulled the keys to the Chrysler out of his pocket and looked at them as if they'd give him the answer. When they didn't, he tossed them onto the table and heaved a deep sigh.

Linda took the keys, and she also examined them, but in a way that a superstitious person would examine a strange talisman. If she found an answer in the keys, Charlie couldn't see it. He stood, immobilized by the thought of what came next. "Now the word is out, Charlie," she finally said just a little more gently than before. "Over and out."

Charlie gave another sigh, looked at the disgusting cobwebs forming on the popcorn acoustic ceiling that needed Lysol, and then muttered, "Okay." A short time later, he found himself sitting on one of the wooden benches at the railroad station across the street, and he didn't remember walking there. He didn't want to remember the whole trip, and wished he has never suggested it.

Linda! How could he even go back to Chicago, knowing she would be there? She was his girl! She saved his life, damn it! Didn't that count for something? It showed she cared. But he had apparently showed her he did not, although he hadn't intended to. How could he fix this?

(NORTHERN NEW MEXICO RAILROAD, AGUA ROJO, 6:35 P.M. MDT)

Such were the thoughts that went through Charlie's mind for the next hour. The sun had set and was making a spectacular red and purple display over the mountains to the west of town, but he didn't notice. He also didn't notice the G-class he'd seen earlier that day drive south, U-turn, and park at the north end of the street. And he particularly didn't notice the Taos County Sheriff's cruiser that had been stopped next to the office after he left Room 213. The deputy, only visible in silhouette, had been watching him since then.

The street light nearest to where he was sitting suddenly triggered, and the sodium vapor lamp burst into action with a buzz like a fly on a bug zapper. It brought him around, and he briefly marveled that there was any municipal street lighting at all in this part of the world. Just then, the cruiser pulled out of the motel, made a wide turn, and glided to a stop in front of his bench. Deputy Schrader rolled down the passenger side window and took a good look, then shook her head. She had taken off the Smoky Bear, and Charlie could see that she had a substantial amount of that dirty blonde rolled and pinned under there. "What?" he finally asked, though not really curious in his depressed state of mind.

"I didn't think you beat your girlfriend, so I guess you and she must have had it out." Charlie didn't respond, but instead stared at the Taos County insignia on the door of the cruiser. Bernie leaned over further, and said, "Don't blame Smitty over at the El Cerro. Him and me go way back. He didn't want to make a call, but he didn't want a beating on his conscience. I guess you could say this was a 'watch and wait.'" When Charlie didn't say anything again, she asked, "Did you get a room?"

Charlie shook his head no.

"Well, you are in a pickle," she observed. "I'm seeing 'No Vacancy' signs on all the shack-up joints in town. And yes, they are all right here on this street. I bet you don't even have wheels."

At that point, he shook off a little of his gloom. "I've still got my cell phone, and my rolling suitcase—which I seem to have left parked outside Linda's room—and I can just hole up here for the night."

"That would be loitering, and you probably don't know that it's supposed to get below freezing tonight then."

Charlie just gave her a quizzical look, and then added, "I've both loitered and frozen before; not necessarily in that order."

"Listen, Komensky! Below freezing at over a mile above sea level isn't like below freezing in Illinois, so you better get in. I've got a little cabin west of here just inside the county line, and you're welcome to sleep on the foldout, if your spine can stand the mattress." Then she added, "If you don't, I'm going to take you in for assault and leaving a suspicious package in a public place. Smitty will back me up."

Once they'd picked up Charlie's battered roll-on and headed west, Bernie mounted a valiant effort to engage him in conversation. She tried talking about the fight he'd had with Linda, but gave up on that subject when he seemed to be getting even more withdrawn. Next, she tried talking about the investigation, reminding him that he'd need to get into Santa Fe and get his investigator's license updated if he were going to continue on it without her. Charlie offered only that he'd think about that tomorrow. On her third volley, she launched questions about his past: Was Linda the first? How long had he been a cop? Was the limp from something in the line of duty? Had he ever lived anywhere but Chicago? What was being a big city cop like?

Charlie's morose mood kept him from seeing the beautiful aftermath of sunset, which Bernie pointed out to him in her fourth line of attack. The sky was a palette of colors with glowing reds and purples in the west and new stars in the east. Then she gave up on the sky and went off talking about mountain hunting trips she'd taken with her father, who had taught her how to use firearms. She'd gotten to a long, and well-rehearsed, script about how her boyfriends had never really liked the outdoors as much as she did, before she realized that the moody cop in the passenger seat had succeeded more in getting her to open up than she had the other way around. She ended with, "But enough about you, Charles Komensky."

Ten minutes of silence later, she took the right turn into a narrow rock-paved drive through heavy spruce and *piñon* pine that led to her cabin. After a steady climb for about three minutes, during which the headlights of the cruiser offered the only light, they rolled out into a clearing. Her cabin sat nested against a foothill—a mountain to Charlie's Midwestern point of view—on an acre of cleared land. The cabin looked like it was built with hand-hewn logs sealed together with a cement-like substance, and Charlie guessed that her loving father had built it to facilitate those hunting trips she talked so much about.

He had been listening, but had not had the energy to engage. As much time as he'd spent on the streets of Chicago and suburbs, he'd never become an outdoorsman, so the surroundings of the little cabin had little immediate significance. He judged by where the glow in the sky remained after sunset that the back of the cabin faced north. On the east side, a little carport had been built, but it was unoccupied by any personal vehicle. At the west perimeter of the clearing, and a little ways up the mountain, he noticed a small metal outbuilding, not unlike a Midwestern garden shed, but taller and skinnier with only a narrow door on it, and no windows. Above the metal shed, on the hill behind the cabin, an old water tank leaned precariously downward. A power line ran to a pole behind the shed, and another line ran from there to the cabin. He thought the shed was a well house, but didn't know for sure. Knowing as little as he did about rural living, he would never have guessed that the muddy puddles of brown liquid he saw at the southwest perimeter of the clearing were from a defective septic system. The ambient light had become low enough that, even with the small bulb burning under the carport, he could look up as he got out of the cruiser and see more stars then he had ever seen before.

He continued to look up as they walked to the front door, the view both fascinating him and making him wish that he were at a place like this with Linda. "Nice place," he ventured. "Your father's?"

"So you were listening. Dad built this cabin in fifty-nine," said Bernie. "He used it until right before he passed away two years ago."

"Sorry."

"Don't be. It was short and sweet. The best you can hope for. Come on in."

Charlie pulled his roll case up the short step and turned to look back for one more moment at the magnificent starlight. The headlights of a vehicle out by the highway, just barely visible through the tree cover, caught his eye. It looked like maybe somebody using the drive as a turnaround, or maybe looking for an address on the dark, rural road, and he didn't give it a second thought.

He took stock of the inside of the cabin as Bernie walked about turning on the few lamps that were the only electric illumination in the place. The overall floor plan was a square, with a large living room—maybe it was a great room—taking up almost the front half of the quadrilateral. Four pieces of primitive pine furniture, a couch with side table, a padded bench, and a chair, occupied the half of the living room to his left, where a large, stone fireplace—seemingly the only heating system in the structure—was the dominating feature. Its flue rose up to the ceiling of rafters, all of which were the same hand-hewn timber as the outside of the cabin, and all of which had been lovingly sanded and finished in a light varnish. Roughly half of the wall area of the living room had been finished in knotty pine plank, the rest in open framing that had been turned—by insertion of horizontal boards—into shelving of sorts. Where no furniture stood, on his right, Charlie saw a magnificent Indian blanket being used as a floor covering. He reasoned that Bernie Schrader was right in not covering it, or damaging it, by putting furniture on it. The pattern, in black, white, and a hue that matched the varnish on the rafters, reminded him of one he'd seen a good twenty years before in an antique shop back home that the shop owner called Two Gray Hills.

In the gloom toward the back of the cabin, he could see a small kitchen that formed an L with the living room. There was a table in a small eating area back there, and the kitchen looked modern enough. Because he saw only one door on each of the interior walls of the L, he assumed that one led to a bedroom and the other to a bathroom, but his mind didn't rule out the possibility that the bathroom was "out back."

On each side of the front door, big picture windows would afford a view of the clearing in front of the cabin and the drive back to the main road. The only window treatments were two Navajo Moki blankets—or copies—that were tacked to the tops of the window frames and pulled to one side with cords to be let loose for a degree of privacy. Bernie saw him looking and answered his unspoken question. "There aren't any close neighbors, so I usually don't let those down, but since you'll be sleeping in here. . . "

"No favors, please."

Bernie went to a small, old refrigerator that had been hand painted with primitive designs not otherwise distinguishable in the dim light, and pulled out two brown bottles labeled as Marble. "Here, quench a little. Let me change out of these cop duds and I'll get us something to eat. I bet you haven't had any food all day."

"Neither have you," he observed.

"Good for my girlish figure," she said, smiling, throwing back her shoulders, and patting her slim belly. She really didn't look as squishy as when he'd first encountered her, and the action served to emphasize her breasts and made her look actually feminine for the first time since they had met.

Charlie rolled his case to a corner near the couch, where he assumed he would be sleeping, and amused himself for the next ten minutes by standing as close to the glass as possible and looking out the picture window. He could still see some of the bright stars despite the interior lamps, and noticed that there was virtually no traffic on the highway. When a vehicle did go by, all that could be seen were quick flashes of the headlights moving like a theater marquee border one way or the other. After a time, he heard her puttering in the kitchen but didn't turn around right away.

By the time he did, she had walked the kitchen table out onto the hardwood floor and into the living room, where she had rolled up the Two Grey Hills and stood it in on end in the front corner. She had also set out two unmatched plates, two coffee cups, and a set of even more unmatched silverware. "Hope you don't mind paper towels for napkins," she said, not looking at him.

"I didn't even want to eat. Remember?"

She had changed into an oversized Denver Broncos t-shirt, a pair of frayed denim shorts that came to just above her knees, and Indian moccasins. Her let down hair was longer than he had expected, reaching under her shoulder blades in back and falling enticingly over now unfettered and substantial bosoms in front. He couldn't help but notice that her nipples showed through the shirt, and made a mental note that nature was a much better architect than bra designers. Just as quickly, the mental picture of Linda, drunk and wine-stained in a cheap motel, reared up from his overactive conscience and dumped him back into the depression bucket.

Bernie put a big steaming bowl of something stew-like and vaguely green into the middle of the table and invited him to sit. She went back to the fridge and came back with two more bottles each of the tolerable local beer. Charlie had already wordlessly seated himself, but, before she sat, she took down a half-empty bottle of *Patrón* and positioned it to one side. "For later," she explained.

They ate silently, Charlie consuming a bowl of the spicy meal, and Bernie eating lightly but downing the beer like a fish. When he asked for seconds and stated, "That's a passable good gumbo," she had to explain that it was green chili stew, made of pork, beef and chicken, and that she made it from an old family recipe that her great-grandmother from Taos Pueblo had used.

"I'll have to get you some of her frybread, too," she offered. Seeing that he was still in the dumps and eating more as a responsibility than enjoying it, she then asked, "Do you want to talk about your girlfriend?"

Charlie took a half-bottle swig and finished the beer—his second—and looked hard at the now lovely young woman who sat across from him. He couldn't tell if she had put on or taken off makeup when she had changed, but something was different. A Mickey Gilley tune quickly ran through his mind. The girls all get prettier at closing time. "My love life is the last thing I should be discussing with you, young lady."

"Not so young," she corrected with a sour face. In a statement that most females wouldn't make until they knew Charlie better, she recounted her birth date. While twisting off the cap on his third beer, Charlie did the math. She was twelve years younger.

Deputy Schrader then recounted a plethora of information of the TMI category about growing up in the mountains and learning to be self-reliant. She had gone to public school in Taos and then taken a year off before getting a pre-law degree from Eastern New Mexico and her certificate from the New Mexico State Police Academy. In her words, she'd been bustin' bad guys ever since. She had two girlfriends in Albuquerque that she saw occasionally, and her last boyfriend had been a "complete asshole." She ended with, "Now spill!" The third beer had loosened him up and made him feel a little more like himself, so he ordered a fourth. "How about a tequila chaser?" she asked as she reached for the bottle. This had been what the coffee cups were for, as he hadn't seen any coffee.

Along about eleven, with Bernie into her second six-pack—she may drink like a fish but she held it like a double-hulled tanker—Charlie had finished his account of being a Chicago cop and graduating to the suburbs where he'd had some success before setting out on his own. He left out that his financial situation was currently in the toilet, but regaled Bernie with a couple of interesting cases, and explained how he did auto salvage sales for insurance companies on the side. At some time between the first tequila and what was to become Charlie's fourth beer, Bernie had tied up the front of her t-shirt bolero style to reveal that her shorts were hip-riders and she had a miniature tattoo of a Glock 7 just under her navel. A tease to the imagination, to be sure, the barrel of the artwork pointed straight down.

Another hour passed, during which Charlie successfully avoided talking or thinking about Linda, and after which he was feeling pretty loose. Bernie had been attentive and didn't seem to be suffering any physical effects from the alcohol. Some of her barbs changed from thoroughly good-natured to something more aggressive. When he told her about how a captain of police had pulled rank on him as to how to proceed on an investigation of a crime wave in the suburbs, she made some remarks about the kind of rock the captain's mother had crawled out from, and the vitriol was real. A few minutes later, she was listening intently when he described a family of meth addicts he had busted, and she burst out with, "Fuck 'em all, Charlie!" She then threw her half-empty beer bottle into the fireplace, where it shattered and splashed into a mess that covered the hearth. He looked back at her and found she was smiling at him, ready to listen to another story.

"I think it's a wash for tonight," he answered, stretching and yawning.

She leaned forward and conspiratorially said, "Komensky, I don't think that bitch appreciates you." He didn't know why, but it started something in him that he felt he wasn't going to be able to control—an inordinate sadness that brought tears to his eyes. "Oops. I've done it now," she stated. "G'nite." She strolled away into the door he'd assumed to be a bedroom, not looking back, and untying the shirt as if she were preparing to pull it off.

Charlie waited for a while, finishing the last beer and thinking about—and rejecting—having another shot of *Patrón*. He half expected her to come back in and make another pass, though the stroll to the bedroom had been signal enough, a signal he wasn't quite in the right mood to obey. Finding a broom in the corner of the kitchen, he swept up the broken glass and some beer with it. He managed to brush his teeth and use the small bathroom, and then stripped to his t-shirt and boxers and settled in on the couch, pulling a knitted Afghan partly over him. Sleep came quickly, and with it a dream in which he and Linda were making love on a moving train in the lower berth of a particularly spacious private room.

(CABIN, TAOS COUNTY, NEW MEXICO, MONDAY, OCTOBER 8, 2:45 A.M.)

He didn't know what woke him up, just that the dream hadn't ended. He remembered that he'd forgotten to turn off the lamps, but the only light now appeared to come from behind him, and from a moon that had risen since he turned in. The moonlight came through the gaps in the picture window that the blankets didn't cover. Kneeling in front of him, Bernie just watched him with tender, dark eyes. She no longer wore the Broncos shirt, and her impressive, naked bosom gently rose and fell in the moonlight with her even breathing. He realized that he was somewhat invested in the dream, and the evidence in the boxer shorts department would be obvious.

Still, like her, he just watched and waited. It was a mutual agreement that this was just something that was happening, and neither wanted to change it. No words necessary. Soon, she seemed to be leaning in closer to him, and he felt her slowly encouraging his arousal. He wanted nothing more in that moment than to kiss her breasts, but before he could act, she stood and removed her shorts, certifying that the Glock tattoo had good aim. He could imagine no more appropriate progression toward love making than what was happening. He sat up. She took off his boxers. The foreplay continued until she reached into a drawer in the small end table at his feet and took out a condom. He realized that he hadn't used a condom in years. Linda didn't approve of them.

It hit him like a high voltage charge. "Linda!" All he could do was extract himself from the situation as quickly as possible and attempt to find his boxers, while Bernie struggled to get her shorts back on.

"It's okay," she said gently. "I'll give you this one, Charlie Komensky. It's not your fault."

What happened next surprised them both. A single rifle shot cracked from outside, almost simultaneously shattering the picture window on the east side of the cabin. The glass blowing out of the center of the window scattered onto the table where they had been sitting a couple of hours earlier, and Charlie heard a piece of dinnerware shatter in the kitchen. Before he could get his wits about him, Bernie had run into the bedroom and come out with her Glock 7. She squatted in a shooters stance, gun pointing out the other window, still naked from the waist up. He long-armed his sport shirt from the back of one of the kitchen chairs, pulled his police .38 out from his roll case, and tossed her the shirt. "Go ahead, you cover up, and I'll cover." She put it on enthusiastically.

Charlie plastered himself against the wall next to the unbroken window and tried to get a peek at the shooter. The moonlight revealed the silhouette of a dark-colored or black crossover type vehicle, probably a late model, parked almost in the middle of the clearing, lights off, facing the house. He couldn't see if the shooter was in it, or somewhere in the trees. "I'm starting to think that first shot was only to get our attention," he whispered. "Does this place have a back door?"

"My bedroom's got a patio door."

"Good. I'm going to chance that the shooter is still out front." He found his pants on top of the roll case handle and got into his shoes. The t-shirt would have to do, as he realized that a lot of cold mountain air was blowing through the hole in the front window.

Before he could get out through the back, a voice yelled from the clearing. "Now that I've got your attention, Deputy, I need to discuss something with you." The voice sounded different, maybe Australia or New Zealand, and close enough to hear them. Bernie looked at him, and Charlie put his finger to his lips and shook his head. Using cop sign language—finger pointing out, finger to forehead, finger pointing to the floor of the cabin, finger showing the number one—Charlie told Bernie that the shooter thought she was alone, and then started for the bedroom.

Bernie followed and whispered, "I can pick him off from in here."

"Shhhh! No! Too dangerous. There may be more than one. Besides, this one wants something from you and doesn't know I'm here."

She grabbed his arm again. "Listen, there's a valve behind the well shack that will release all of the water in the old tank. I use it to flush out the septic system. Whoever it is parked that vehicle right on top of it and doesn't know it. If you flush it with that weight on it, the walls of the old cistern will collapse and drop that hot crossover into the muck like a trap door opening. Maybe then we can get the drop on them and find out what they want."

Charlie reasoned that, one enemy or more, that wasn't a bad idea. In the confusion they could probably get the upper hand. But, before they could act, the headlights of the dark vehicle went on and flooded the open side of the living room with light. They wouldn't be able to see much in that direction except for the glare. Then, from outside, came the voice, "That's your signal to decide, Deputy Schrader. I wasn't planning on being here all night. Got me a plane to catch." The headlights blinked twice. The man, at least at that moment, was at or near the vehicle; and he had referred to himself in the singular.

"I trust your judgment," Charlie said to Bernie, and hustled out the back.

When she had gotten where she thought was good cover, even if the assailant could figure the direction of her voice, she yelled, "Deputy Bernice Schrader, Taos County Sheriff here. Put down your gun and come forward with your hands up."

The answer came as a shot that shattered the other window and took down the blanket from over it. "You come out with your hands up," said the strange voice.

In back of the cabin, Charlie had a hard time finding the valve. Despite the moonlight, the cabin was throwing a prodigious shadow on the hillside, and he stumbled over odd objects several times. The lights of the dark vehicle going on didn't help, just making the adjustment to the total darkness of the shadows even worse. Additionally, his leg was acting up, and trying to balance on the steep hillside wasn't helping. Finally, he banged his shin on a hard, immovable object just below the tank. Feeling for his shin with one hand and for the valve with the other, he had to sit down onto the rock and take a breath. After he heard the "voice" order Bernie out with her hands up, he hoped she hadn't taken him up on it.

It took all his might to turn the damn valve. He struggled to find something to use for a lever, then gave up on that and braced both legs against the footings of the cabin and put all his weight into it. A satisfying gurgle from the tank seemed to signify success.

Bernie, too, heard the gurgle that she recognized as the water tank emptying into the cistern, but she had another problem: The man with the voice was now lunging at the front door, trying to open it. So much for dumping him into the cistern with his vehicle. Her academy training kicked in. If she shot through the door, it would be murder for sure, as she couldn't tell if he was still armed. If she didn't shoot, she'd have to wait until he burst through and take her chances. "I thought you just wanted to talk," she yelled.

"Too late, mate." The explosion of splinters from the door hit her in the face and startled her. More police training: This was imminent danger of life and limb. Her first shot went wide and hit the wall. Before she could re-aim, he jumped her and knocked the Glock out of her hand, sending it flying into the bedroom. In a flash, he had her in a headlock with a small Luger pointed at her head. "Be reasonable, Chickie, and I won't put a plug in you—yet."

"I don't know what you want," she offered, still looking for a physical way out. She knew that the cistern would take time to fill up, and she didn't know how much time she had, or whether Charlie would come back in the front or the back.

"You been holdin' out on a little evidence, back there were you found that stiff."

How would he know that? Unless he had someone inside her department, or the OMI's office. She tried an elbow to his ribs, but in response he pulled her up so that he had her in front of him with his strong arm around her neck. This time, he brought the Luger up under her loose shirt and pointed it under her chin. "I don't know . . . what you're . . . talking about," she gasped as she felt the cold metal of the weapon and his gun hand against her breasts.

"All we want is for you to turn in that little stone so that it becomes part of the evidence, get me? If it's money you're after, I'll see you get paid."

"We still don't know what you're talking about." Charlie's voice came from the bedroom, confusing the attacker, but he tightened his grip on her and faced the bedroom, holding her as a shield. "Show yourself or Deputy Chickie dies, and I find what I'm looking for on her body. Wouldn' mind feelin' around a bit on that, eh?"

"She doesn't have it." Charlie moved just far enough into the light that his face could be seen. He knew that the attacker, who he could now see was dressed head to toe in leather and was wearing a leather ski mask over his head, would have the same trouble he had just experienced in adjusting to the shadows created by the vehicle headlights.

"Who then? You?" Just then, a sound like somebody dumping rocks down a metal chute came from the clearing. The lights from the vehicle simultaneously lifted, then went out completely, as it fell into the collapsing cistern. The attacker apparently thought the sound was a threat out front and struggled to turn his Luger outward from under Bernie's shirt. Without hesitation, Bernie got her left arm up and over and knocked the Luger out of the attacker's hand. As Charlie moved to be sure he had it safely in hand, she pulled a police MA move and neatly flipped the assailant over on top of the table. He landed with a crack and a grunt, but the table didn't give. The blow had snapped something, and he lay flailing his arms and apparently unable to move his legs.

"I'll call the guys," she said, smiling at Charlie. "Thanks." She smiled broadly but softly, a true expression of gratitude. He could have—should have—picked her up, hugged her and kissed her right there. But something told him that was a bad idea.

CHAPTER FOUR

(CABIN, TAOS COUNTY, NEW MEXICO, OCTOBER 8, 6:45 A.M.)

By the time the investigation wound up, the sky was rewinding its after-sunset spectacular from the night before. Both Charlie and Bernie were cold and hungry; lighting a fire in the big fireplace after the cops released the cabin with both front windows still blown out was like trying to deep fry an ice cube. The sheriff had made a judgment call—probably a good one—and had asked the State Police to handle it; because the assault involved an off-duty deputy. Both of them, one at a time, had gone back into the cabin to identify the man sans ski mask. Besides the angry, blue eyes, nothing about his cleft chin, triangular face, and broad forehead seemed familiar to either of them. He was only slightly less angry, and in excruciating pain, when they airlifted him to University Hospital in Albuquerque. His only words, besides asking to talk to a lawyer, would've made a sailor blush and a pornographer rethink his script.

They both cleaned up as best they could, and, once the black G-class was removed from the cistern, Bernie made a long phone call to her headquarters to get all the information she could get on the case scribbled into her notebook. She also got a dispensation to drive Charlie to Santa Fe to hook up with the licensing people and the OMI. It was ten by the time they got packed up and she managed to maneuver her police cruiser through the mud around the cistern and down to the drive. As they pulled out onto the main road, Charlie, feeling more talkative than the night before, offered his condolences. "Sorry about your cabin."

She shrugged it off. "My boss is going to have some boys from Taos come over and replace the glass. I'll clean up the rest later, but I'll have to save up a little more money before I can pay for a new cistern. Guess I'll have them put in a portable crapper."

Bernie had managed to convert herself back into Deputy Schrader, and Charlie had done just a change of sport shirt, from green to off white, and had on the same blue Dockers. In deference to the unexpected warmth of the sun that morning, he left the shirt un-tucked and open three buttons down in front. Glancing her way, he asked, "Has anyone ever talked to you about the Jekyll and Hyde thing you've got going with that blue uniform shirt?"

She looked down at her shirt, and then realized what he was talking about and took it good naturedly. "It's called a sports bra. You should try it sometime."

He realized that he was displaying his physique—the only word Charlie could ever bring himself to use when describing a man's chest—and responded in kind, "What you get is all me, all the time."

As he did so, she pulled her notebook out of her shirt pocket and tossed it into Charlie's lap. "Take a look at my last notes. You'll see they identified the guy from the cabin."

Flipping open the tabbed page, he saw that the man with the Australian accent was tentatively identified as Nick Bermuda. They'd found an Illinois DL in his back pocket and checked the lodger's association, finding him checked out from a hotel in Los Alamos. In the sludge-drenched car, they'd found, of all things, a German passport, suggesting that his real name might be Nicholas Ramunda, a name that had mob connections on both the east and west coasts and possibly in Europe. "How does somebody with a Sicilian name and an Australian accent wind up with a German passport?" he asked, but Bernie didn't have an easy answer. He suggested she have her chief find out whether there were any photographs of the guy as Nicholas Ramunda available, no matter how old, assuming that the photograph on his license and passport matched the guy now awaiting back surgery in the hospital.

"How long until we get to Santa Fe?"

"Another fifty or so. Why?" She took her foot off the gas. "You got something in mind?"

"Nothing concrete. Just keep driving. I just thought we ought to use the time to go over what we know." Accelerating again, she suggested that Charlie start the discussion. "I'd rather hear it from your point of view. Fresh perspective," he said, waiting for her to begin.

"Well. I'm no homicide detective, but it seems to me that Bermuda—or Ramunda—is a suspect. His verbalizations back at the cabin suggest involvement. Other than that, we've got a stiff in a bag that was killed somehow, dragged to the railroad, disposed of in a manner that's indicative of a message killing—and that means shot after death—it's either message or some damn hateful revenge. Then there's Ramunda's urgent need to have some kind of evidence exposed. It seems to support a message killing for hire theory. It's possible he doesn't get paid unless the full message is sent." She looked at Charlie in a way that said, "How am I doing so far?"

(STATE OFFICE COMPLEX, SANTA FE, NEW MEXICO,
MONDAY, OCTOBER 8, ALMOST NOON MDT)

Charlie's reason and logic took a direct hit when he saw the name of the head of the state's application review board on the directory:

PATRICIA DEFOY-GRASS - ROOM 230

"Is this for real?" he asked himself. "Does anybody just stand in front of a mirror and pronounce their names anymore?" He also asked himself whether he wanted to call her Patty or Paté if he got pissed off at her. He continued asking himself during a forty minute wait, reasoning that it no longer would take much to reach pissed status. He was still asking himself when he found out she had gone to a late lunch without seeing him and would be back at one. Unfortunately, her secretary failed to tell Charlie this until a quarter to one, making it impossible for him to leave the building and seek out a lunch himself. There had been no breakfast at the cabin, and getting hungrier by the minute really pissed him off.

Another forty-five minutes later, at 1:30, he was admitted to an austere office that looked like it had been furnished in the 1950s and introduced to one Cindy Vigil. "Ms. Defoy's Assistant for Interstate Affairs," the secretary explained.

"Vee Hill, you say?" It was at this point that he knew he was being jerked around. He looked at the placard on her desk and, offering a hand, said, "Pleased to meet you Miss Viggle." The mutilation of her name didn't phase her, so after she told him that his application for a new license had been denied due to not meeting the statutory requirements, he blew up.

"Listen, kid. No offense, but I've been a cop and a private investigator since before somebody was wiping the asses of your grandparents. I'm just trying to get an endorsement to handle something while I'm visiting your fine state."

"Ms. Defoy has spoken on this," the kid replied, not just a little hesitantly.

"I guarantee that some regulatory hack isn't going to be the last word. When can I see her?"

"She has left for a meeting."

Charlie flicked his hand in her direction. "You go tell her—because you and I both know that she hasn't left—that I'm going over her head." When she hesitated, he flicked again. "Just go and do whatever you do to make yourself look old enough to have this job, and leave me to make a phone call."

"You should . . . "

Charlie held up his hand in a stopping gesture. "I'll cover you, now go!" She closed the door behind her.

"Who does a guy have to shoot to make a buck around here," he mumbled as he pulled out his cell and dialed his mentor, Judge Elmo Burmeister. He reached the judge on the second try, at a political brunch somewhere on Chicago's north side. After explaining the situation and the roadblocks he was getting from state government, he closed the flip phone with a satisfied look and sat back. Looking around the room, he hoped he hadn't stepped on the wrong toes. Any state that was hard up enough for cash to use furniture this old had to have politicians that were on the take. There was just no other explanation. It reminded him way too much of his home venue of Chicago.

A knock interrupted his thoughts about what nice kindling the furniture would make. "Come in!" A striking brunette, tall and slim and wearing a long leather skirt over brown, high-heeled boots, a light linen blouse with an Indian motif down the front, and turquoise jewelry consisting of a heavy necklace and wide bracelets on both wrists came in. She had apparently tried to put on an angry face before coming in, but the sight of Charlie—relaxed in spite of the situation—caused a twinkle in her brown eyes and a slight smirk on her full lips. She was made up for business, handsome but not romantically beautiful, and had some features that Charlie identified as clearly of Hispanic or Native American origin. In the event that she had to go before television cameras, only a slight touchup would make her ready. She carried a leatherbound folder in what Charlie saw as "girl's way," but nothing else. Charlie stood up to greet her.

With her right hand extended in such a way that her fingers—together in a bundle - pointed at his waist and her extravagantly manicured thumb pointed at his chest, she said, "Patricia DeFoy-Grass. Mister Komensky?"

He put on his best Gomer Pyle. "Awful glad to meet ya." He shook her hand vigorously and hoped that the extra hard grip he used broke a nail. "Awful glad."

She gave him a look that told him she knew it was sarcasm but would go with it anyway. "Let's get down to business, shall we." Without asking him to sit, she pulled a smaller manila folder out of the leatherbound. "Let me first apologize for my reticence in agreeing to meet with you on short notice. It's not every day that I get a walk-in with someone who has as much, er, pull—for lack of a better word—as you do."

Now he saw her expression as a look of admiration and just a little jealousy, and that from a political hack who probably wasn't even on the bigwigs' fundraiser list yet. Charlie usually had little time or need for sycophants, but knew that cultivating connections never hurt. "Miz Defoy," he responded, shunning his inner urge to call her Duck Liver.

"I would only ask that you show me the respect of letting me conduct my important business in your impressive state."

"Now who's buttering who, Mr. Komensky." She handed him the manila folder. "I think you will find that the governor has endorsed an administrative exception for your Illinois license, granted you a temporary concealed carry, and requested that you keep her informed about the results of your investigation. Just between you and me, I'd like know how you pulled this off."

"If I told you . . . "

"Yes, I know, you'd have to shoot me."

"I was going to say take you to lunch. Now that I'm back on the case, I have some questions for you, and I didn't have breakfast." He knew she couldn't say no. Not with the political ambition glowing behind those fascinating dark eyes.

The gourmet lunch chosen by Miss Defoy-Grass, in a quaint looking little restaurant just off the historic plaza, was not and had never been in Charlie's budget. To him, the place was a run-down shack that should have been bulldozed before the Spanish American War, and the portions wouldn't satisfy a hamster. In fact, a hamster would demand better. But he managed to pump her for information about any rumors she might have heard, political or otherwise, about anyone in Taos County, the State Police, or the Office of Medical Investigator being hooked up with organized crime. "And not the 'dump the body in Juarez' kind, but the 'horse head in the bed' kind," he pointed out. The only thing she knew was that the Indians were up to their gonads in gambling, and it had been rumored that some Vegas types had occasionally strong-armed members of the tribes. She rejected that anyone in State Police or OMI was connected, but couldn't rule out the county.

"Would you take the opportunity, if it meant getting invited to one of those fundraisers?" he asked. He meant it, too, because she just seemed too intrigued with the subject of what anyone would get in return for helping out 'The Mafia.'

"Does the mob enforcer look like you," she returned coyly. "And is that how you manage to get around the rules?"

"Would I be asking if I was connected?"

She looked disappointed. "I suppose not. You would probably just go about your business without taking the trouble to get a license. So how did you do it?"

"Trade secret, but I will tell you this, sweetheart. You got to stop using people to climb over, and start letting them climb with you." He knew he had read her when she looked crestfallen, and he rose to leave. "Forgive me if I don't walk you back to that retro building. I've got to rent a car and get to Albuquerque, that's why I took my roll case."

(SANTA FE PLAZA, OCTOBER 8, 2:30PM MDT)

Finding an agency right on the plaza, Charlie managed to get a rental car. Of the three available without a reservation, he picked a Ford Mustang, with which he'd had prior experience. While waiting for the paperwork on the car, he reviewed the contents of the manila. A letter from the governor would serve as his introduction in any state agency, but another letter was addressed to him in a separate, sealed envelope. He opened it and read it with some concern, because he didn't want to get his good friend and mentor, Judge Burmeister, into any hot water. It said:

Dear Mr. Komensky: As governor, It is my heartfelt wish that you be able to properly conduct your business while you are a guest of the great State of New Mexico. My desire to have you complete your business with a positive outcome is not entirely altruistic. Your business appears to be the people's business, by reason of the State of New Mexico having a half interest in the railroad upon which was committed a heinous crime. While I have not had the time to consult with all of my contacts in law enforcement, I have been assured by the Hon. Elmo Burmeister that this crime may involve organized crime of a nature for which we, in New Mexico, have no tolerance. All I ask in return is that you keep me informed of significant developments in a timely fashion. As such, please use Ms. Patricia Defoy-Grass as your exclusive liaison. She has my ultimate trust in this regard. Should that contact fail, my office has instructions to give you my limited government cellphone number. Please use it only in a case of extreme need. Your humble servant: T. N.

Just as he finished reading the letter, the porter brought up his rental. "Classy dame, this governor," he said to himself. "I hope her confidence in Duck Liver isn't misplaced."

He managed to find the Office of Medical Investigator, which was scrunched into a far corner of the University of New Mexico Hospital complex, just past four in the afternoon. The drive had been leisurely, a quick sprint south from Santa Fe on Interstate 25, but Charlie found out that it was about twenty degrees hotter in Albuquerque than in Santa Fe. He also had difficulty finding a parking space that didn't appear to be reserved, and finally, in a panic to see what they'd found out about the cause of death before the sidewalks rolled up, parked amongst the empty spaces at the far corner of a "B Lot", the significance of which appeared to be that huge pieces of orange paper would be glued to your windshield if you parked for longer than ten minutes.

The tour of the campus Charlie had given himself while trying to find a parking space didn't make for any improvement in his disposition. He wanted to get this over with early enough to get out of town the next day, and the results would tell him where he would be headed. If nothing else pointed in a different direction, he knew he wanted to get back to Chicago and talk to someone in the Jeweler's Building to learn more about the stone that still rattled around in his pants pocket. The campus seemed to have the kind of split personality that he now knew he would see a lot if he stayed in New Mexico much longer. The buildings on campus didn't know if they were Pueblo Revival, Pueblo Moderne, 20th Century Revival, or just something that had been in the same spot for so long that nobody knew what kind of architecture it was. In any case, they were all a stucco salesman's paradise. Even the newest parts of the hospital complex seemed to have been built to some architectural whim he had never seen before now; call it something between the superstructure of a cruise liner and the grille of a '66 Cady—and this included the new OMI building.

The grad student in white coat and sneakers, with jeans and a t-shirt identifying a defunct rock bank underneath, had little or no interest in serving the public. He gestured Charlie to the second floor, never looked at his ID, and never really looked up from the obscure medical text in which he seemed engrossed. Charlie guessed that the OMI's office didn't get many personal visits, as all business with the families of deceased individuals would likely be done by police or funeral directors. The other way would be too stressful and disruptive for scientific enquiry. On this basis, he also assumed that most visitors were likely physicians, messengers, or connected to law enforcement in one way or the other. By the time he'd finished climbing the wide, open staircase to the second floor, his bad leg bothered him and he knew that he was getting too close to the end of the day to expect it to get any better.

Unlike facilities of this kind he was used to, the floor was laid out with enough glass in the partitions to see that the OMI investigator's offices were clustered on both sides of a central examining or autopsy room. The latter probably was not glassed quite as much, in respect for the deceased, and for any confidential medical information that could be gleaned by anyone who just stood around where he was at that moment. Before he could decide what to do next, Sam Speeno strolled out of one of the offices. From his neck to the bottoms of his feet, he wore protective gear of the kind Charlie expected to see in a contagious disease ward. A plastic covering like a shower cap covered his head where the Tyrolean hat had been the day before. He peeled off rubber gloves and found a disposal point, marked with the familiar biohazard symbol, in the wall, and then he walked toward Charlie. With a smile, he said, "This is not what I would have expected, so you are either considerably more resourceful or considerably more dimwitted, and I credited you with neither."

Immediately thinking of the possibility of a mole in the OMI's office, Charlie countered, "Hoping that I'd be thrown off the case?"

"I will not be the one to complain to the authorities if you are not properly licensed to question me, I will simply tell you that I am not allowed to answer your questions."

"I'll go back to the car and get my paperwork."

Speeno grabbed his arm. "I said I would tell you I am not allowed. I didn't say I wouldn't. Come and sit with me." Never letting go of Charlie's arm, Speeno guided him to an office with a small desk that was strewn with papers and photographs, as was every other piece of furniture in the room. He gestured again for Charlie to push the paperwork aside and have a seat.

"Where's your magic stick?"

"It is an affectation I prefer to use only when I am . . . out of range."

"Of what, your bosses?"

"I prefer to think of them as intrusions in the job at hand, but you should not assume that I give them any less respect than they are due."

Charlie laughed, and then said, "That's just a way of saying that they may not be due much."

Seeming to ignore Charlie, the MI rummaged through the pictures on his desk. "Ah," he finally exclaimed. "Here it is! This is the cause of death."

Charlie took the glossy file print and squinted at it. It appeared to Charlie to show a pinprick in skin, surrounded by some scattered light bruising or hemorrhaging under the skin. Recognizing it immediately as the telltale pattern from a hastily used inoculation gun, Charlie looked back at Speeno, who was smiling and leaning back in his chair with his hands folded over his chest. "Was our stiff in the military? Or planning to leave on a trip so a tropical country?"

"I doubt the former, and I don't have any physical evidence to support the latter. But, as you can see, that was the delivery system."

Charlie's mind started working the facts. "So somebody knew that our stiff was going to be getting a shot for some reason, and arranged to put a poison into the inoculation gun. What was it?"

"That's the interesting part. I've searched the literature, and I have not found any murders committed using this particular agent. And the irony is sublime, considering where Mr. Ortega and his men found the body. It's boiler wash."

"Well, almost, but not exactly boiler wash. The trace chemicals we found in the blood of the deceased suggest the decomposition products of something called DBNPA. It is a chemical made largely for the use of the power plant industry, but I would suppose, just for the sake of argument that perhaps our fine narrow gauge railroad uses it in their tenders. You know, the tank that supplies water to the steam locomotive."

"Yes, I know," said Charlie impatiently. He knew that Speeno had no reason to know how much Charlie knew about the details of steam railroading.

The MI squinted at him and went on. "Our weapon of choice does afford some benefit by keeping the scale off the insides of boilers, but its primary use, the one for which it is intended by the manufacturer, is as a biocide."

"So you're saying it kills biological material?"

"Do not run so far ahead of me that I can't catch up, Mr. Komensky. It prevents formation of algae and mold, and generally does not have a deleterious effect on mammals when mixed with that much water."

"Then?"

"I'm getting to it, and will be around to my salient point in just a moment. First, do you know how many inoculations have to be injected directly into a patient's bloodstream?"

"I couldn't even guess."

"They are few and far between, Mr. Komensky. And rarely would those that are common be injected by an inoculation gun. The preferred method would be a drip."

"But you're saying that this stuff, this boiler wash, was directly injected?"

"It got me started thinking." With this, Speeno tapped the top of his shower cap with one finger. "Injection devices are usually subcutaneous. That means . . . "

"I know what it means."

"Right. So if some cleverly diabolical rat of a man found a way to project a long needle with the deadly drug into the vein closest to where the shot was being administered, the victim might scarcely know it. However, the person administering the deadly shot would have to have a very good knowledge of human anatomy, and even then, it might result in a miss. They were taking a chance, and perhaps it just happened to work. Perhaps they have tried it on other people, and failed."

"So what does this boiler wash do if it gets in the bloodstream?"

Speeno shuffled around among some papers until he found what looked like a materials data sheet. "According to the chemical company that made it, it decomposes readily at body temperature. Because decomposition of DBNPA is exothermic—that means it gives off heat—and in so doing raises the temperature of the blood. I am convinced that the poisonous effects of this biocide are negligible when ingested through the stomach. The stomach is used to handling hot food. But the body can't readily counteract the effects of heat already in the blood. The brain will be damaged irreparably if the temperature shoots up high enough. The result will be no different than a subdural hematoma. The victim may have experienced only momentary disorientation before passing out."

"How long does this take?"

Raising an index finger upward to indicate that Charlie should again wait, Speeno shuffled through more paperwork. Finding what he needed, he answered, "Calculations based on the normal rate of decomposition of DNBPA at 98.6 degrees Farenheit say that our victim probably had only five minutes."

Charlie whistled. "Five minutes? That means that, if our perp is a doctor . . . "

"Don't assume, Mr. Komensky, that the perpetrator was a doctor. There are many places other than a medical clinic where this man could have gone to get a shot, even some on the black market. The Russians, I believe, are still particularly fond of using old-fashioned inoculation guns for mass inoculations. Also, if I were you, I would argue that the perpetrator had little confidence in the DNBPA actually working, which would explain a later bullet, just to be sure."

"Or to throw us off." It certainly wasn't out of the question that a Russian would be involved in something like diamond smuggling, so Charlie tried to reason out a kill scenario in his head before asking the MI any more questions. Charlie had heard rumors that the Russian FSB trained its agents where to shoot so that you got a through and through, making recovery of the slug by the assassin easier than digging it out of the target. Perhaps the lawyer had represented someone who had stolen from a Russian, and he was killed to send a message that the Russian wanted his diamonds back. The stone in Charlie's pocket was worth a lot to an average guy, but to a Russian who dealt in stones by the carload, it would have been a small price to pay to send an important message. But why a steam locomotive? Unless the message was being sent to a railroad fan like Charlie himself. He combed his memory to think of any cases he had in his long career that would make the message for him. But if for him, why was Nick Ramunda so concerned that the message had not been sent? Or was the whole idea of sending a message a "wrong track," so to speak?

Without realizing his train of thought was gelling, he asked Speeno, "Do you have any experts in gemstones?"

"Are you buying or selling?" The MI gave Charlie a look that said he didn't quite understand the question, but would go along. This told Charlie two things: It was unlikely Speeno was involved in the crime, and he should shut up now. "Never mind."

CHAPTER FIVE

(ALVARADO TRANSPORTATION CENTER, ALBUQUERQUE, NEW MEXICO, TUESDAY, OCTOBER 9, 10:30 A.M. MDT)

A beautiful fall Tuesday in Albuquerque wasn't much different, in terms of weather, than a late summer Tuesday in Chicago. At least that's what Charlie thought as he sat on a sunlit bench on the track side of the Alvarado Transportation Center waiting for the eastbound Chief. In his element—meaning railroads and trains—he eased back into a slouch, checked again that his roll case was clipped to his belt in case he fell asleep and somebody tried to grab it, and looked around him for the third or fourth time. In its heyday, this platform would have been the stopping point for the very best passenger trains that the Atchison, Topeka and Santa Fe had to offer, and a place where the rich and famous would have gotten off the train to stretch, shop for Indian jewelry, tip a Redcap to run into the Alvarado hotel for booze, or just enjoy the clean, clear, fresh air. In his imagination, he could see the Super Chief stopped there still; four or six magnificent Alco diesels wearing a war bonnet paint scheme, followed by fluted steel-sided postal cars, baggage cars, sleeping cars, lounges and diners, and the dome car with the famous Turquoise Room and its private dining area for up to fourteen people. Further back in time, there would have been a giant steam locomotive, a standard gauge

Northern perhaps, oil-fired and hot, that had just rolled off the turntable at the roundhouse south of town, to replace an engine of similar type, in an orchestrated relay race of heavyweight Pullman cars across the country from Los Angeles to Chicago and back.

In his mind, a scorched and steaming corpse interrupted his reverie by falling out of the front of the locomotive. It disturbed him. To Charlie, it was perhaps the most troubling part of this case; that someone would disrespect an honorable and historic piece of railroad equipment by stuffing a dead body into it. When he came back to reality, only a commuter train with a giant bird painted on the sides of the engine and cars occupied the track in front of him. Talk about disrespect for railroad equipment! With all this going on in his head, Charlie couldn't have comprehended even the possibility that he would have to be right back here following a lead at this same train station before the case was over and the murder solved.

More troubling, but also proof that somebody with connections, maybe inside police connections, or just a lot of power, was his visit to University Hospital the night before. He'd tried to get in to see Nicholas Ramunda. Initially met by a stone wall, he then witnessed a comical flurry of incredulous cover-your-butt activity as the staff and nurses realized what had happened. Ramunda had been released, with all the paperwork necessary to keep from red flagging the system, but no record of who ordered the release. He immediately placed a call to Bernice, who was as surprised as he was—or at least she said she was—and would look into it. She seemed to be all business as she told him that, back at the scene if the crime, they had come up empty on anyone seeing the body dumped. With so many cars moving to and from the station site, and most of them from out of state, people in the area had gotten used to ignoring strange vehicles. The description of both Ramunda and the G-series had been circulated to no avail.

On the State Police side, the DNA lab had confirmed some complete strands that matched nobody in CODIS or NDIS, including Ramunda. Speeno had told him that getting evidence from the burned and smoked body would be iffy, at best. That Ramunda was in the database was interesting, but not conclusive for any of Charlie's far-flung theories.

"How about Ramunda's gun?" he asked. Ramunda should have been smart enough to be sure that the gun had not been involved in any criminal shootings, but he had to confirm.

"It's a clean shooter." She also told him the State Police had had no luck in determining where victim Dinwiddie had been spending his time in New Mexico. No cell phone had been found on the body, no keys, nothing to tie him to a particular location, and no telephone records with his name on them after his last appearance in California over two years before. The landlord for his final law office after he'd left his partners had thought his attorney files to be abandoned and of no value, so he burned them. Convenient! Dinwiddie had never re-applied for the bar in any other state, and fell completely off the radar. Charlie's first thought was that Dinwiddie already knew somebody was, or would be after him when he disappeared. Was he a member of a criminal gang whose other members had also disappeared, perhaps with the loot? That would explain the message thing.

So with Ramunda in the wind, no new or valuable information to be had in Albuquerque, and no Linda to spend an evening with, Charlie had slept, fitfully, in a hotel bed that didn't need the coin-op vibrator to make it move, and spent the morning reserving a last-minute space on Amtrak 4, calling some friends with connections in Chicago—he couldn't very well call Linda—and taking a circumferential walk around the remains of the giant Santa Fe railroad shop complex that had once been a vibrant part of Albuquerque's economy.

When would the Chief get there? He glanced to his right along the track toward the shop complex. Preservationists had mercifully left two of the shop buildings standing, but the turntable was long gone and the shop floors, where once had echoed the deafening clang and clank of boiler work, were vacant and covered with enough desert dust to leave footprints rivaling a moon landing.

(ALBUQUERQUE, TUESDAY, OCTOBER 9, 2:52 P.M. MDT)

Charlie's luck, or the lack of it, held for his trip back to Chicago. The Chief got in just late enough for the diner to be closed, and the first announcement he heard was that the grille in the kitchen had gone down and all that would be available for supper would be the pre-prepped meals. His end of the car, the one with the bedrooms, turned out to be the end where the air conditioning worked the least. Despite the time of year, the high desert sun beating on metal and coming through windows, no matter how well protected, put a substantial heat load on the at least twenty-year-old passenger cars. He slept through La Junta and didn't get a chance to walk, so by the next morning his bad leg ached terribly. No grille meant a pretty crappy breakfast, east of Kansas City, of microwaved pork sausages and an egg of dubious heritage, with a side of toaster waffles and coffee. Charlie thought the coffee always good on board a train, and kept himself awake most of the day by downing cup after cup. He suspected the egg to have come from a milk carton and microwaved long enough to solidify and turn a little rubbery around the edges. Thinking about the possible ways to ruin a hamburger patty, he didn't attempt lunch.

(WEDNESDAY, OCTOBER 10, 6:30PM CDT)

Despite the coffee, Charlie fell asleep somewhere after Galesburg, Illinois, and was awakened by the sound of his superliner car being dragged through the puzzle of switches approaching Union Station, Chicago. Bu-bu-bu-bump – count to three – double bu-bu-bu-bump and repeat. He'd ridden the train into Union Station often enough to know the cadence. Looking out of his window, he determined that the train had just crossed under Roosevelt Road and the sun had set about fifteen minutes before. This also meant that the train was about three hours late. He leaned back to watch the fascinating parade of sights; the train would soon pass under several buildings, into the cave that was the south approach to the station, and through a maze of columns, platforms, switches and other trains until it arrived at end of track. But the next sound didn't bode well.

This time it went bu-bu-bu-bang, followed by a twanging sound like the rending or twisting of heavy steel, then a shudder and vibration that he felt deep into his bones, and a last grinding sound as the car lurched to a stop and started to lean about six degrees to his side of the juke box. "Derailment," he thought. "Just peachy." That the lights in the car went out after the noise stopped, and that he had trouble getting the sliding door of his room open at that angle didn't surprise him. People were already mumbling and filling the narrow aisle of the car, and he decided that, if he was going to see his jewelry expert that evening, he'd have to grab his roll case and get off out there on the approach tracks. Hot footing it across a dozen active tracks during late evening rush would be difficult, but not impossible. But getting out presented a different problem: The superliner cars had all except the family/accessible bedrooms on the upper level where Charlie had so-called economy bedroom. He'd have to bully his way past the ever-increasing population of the single corridor, get down the narrow stairs, and, with no power in the car, find a way to hand crank the sliding doors open. He wished he'd studied more of a book a friend once gave him about Superliner cars. He half considered kicking out one of the emergency exit windows that were clearly marked from the inside of the car, but figured that would attract too much attention. He didn't even like the risk of exiting the car without permission at the scene of a derailment, but with everyone in the car in a state of semi-panic, calculated the odds were better. Remembering that he was the second car from the rear of the train, something about the situation started to nag at him. Why did it seem only his car had derailed? Had someone deliberately thrown one of the puzzle switches right under the car?

The answer burst into his brain in the form of recognizable gunshots—three of them—coming from on the ground on his side of the car. First, for a count of two, everything went quiet. Then shrieking and screaming voices from the center of the car—where the doors are—were followed by multiple, frightened voices yelling, "They shot him!" True to form, passengers began acting out the familiar mob mentality: Half the people wisely surging back up the stairs from the lower level and the other half stupidly pushing down the aisle toward the stairs to stupidly verify with their own eyes that which had already been described. Somebody was shot!

Charlie thought, "Either this is an old fashioned train robbery, or I'm in serious shit." No time to worry about DHS. He pushed past an old woman in the aisle and lunged, with his case, into the middle of the room across the hall. Pulling with all his might on the red handle that invited him to do so IN CASE OF EMERGENCY, he quickly stripped the window gasket out and pushed the hinged portion of the clear Lexan outward. He looked back into the aisle, and could tell by the look on the old woman's face that the gunman—or men—had reached the upper level. This was going to be hell on his bad leg, but it had to be. He lifted his roll case over the sill and dropped it onto the ground. It broke with a sickening crunch. He managed to get out legs-first and hold onto the sill with both hands so that the drop for him would be only five feet or so. Just going down, his last glimpse of the aisle included a man with a sawed off shotgun, maybe five-five, dirty looking, swarthy in a mean way, and wearing a soft, weather-beaten cloth hat and a khaki windbreaker. A metal crown glinted on a tooth in his lower jaw just as the gunman turned toward the open window, Charlie's now vacant window, and realized it was open.

On the ground and breathing heavily, Charlie now had no doubt that the gunman sought him and him alone. He grabbed his case, which was battered but miraculously latched, and threw it under his left arm. The ambient lighting, mostly from surrounding rail service facilities, was sufficient for Charlie to see that the leading truck, the front pair of axles, of the superliner had gone off the tracks and onto the ground, and that his assailants weren't sufficiently versed in railroad safety. Apparently having derailed the train using a heavy pry bar, one of the perps lay almost cut in half and literally spilling his guts where he had been thrown under the truck, like flying off a giant see-saw, by the enormous momentum of the impact of the bar with the moving wheels. Fatally dumb assholes or not, these men had known exactly which car he was on! He tried to think quickly; how many men would he use if he were designing this operation?

There were at least two still after him: One man with a sawed-off and another person who had taken three shots with a handgun and hit somebody. And criminals weren't necessarily logical; this was a poorly designed operation. If you want to derail a train, steal a "derail" if you have to, but a pry bar from a constructions site . . .? By this time, he'd made it to the rear of the train and turned to look back to where the window hung open. Seeing a glint of light that he took to be from dental work, he ran around the back of the last car— right into the muzzle of a Colt .38. He decided that freezing in place was a good idea, and hoped that he hadn't startled the gun's owner enough that the next sound he heard would be his last. But his luck held. Letting his eyes focus in the shadows, he saw a woman—a really big woman—about 6 feet in height, athletic, with short blonde hair and a not unpleasant face: Clear skin, rosy cheeks, smooth lips, slightly rounded but steely grey eyes that told him they could look right through him. She wore a charcoal cloth windbreaker buttoned at the waist and revealing a burgundy camisole underneath; heaving breasts, pure white skin; heavy breathing; tight black jeans and sensible track shoes; heaving breasts again. "Hey, eyes up here," she said throatily.

Charlie continued to breathe heavily himself, though he wasn't that winded. He needed the time to strategize, and to give the other perps a chance to show themselves, so he just froze in a slight crouch with his good leg doing the heavy bracing. If he figured right, there had to be one other armed party holding a gun on the passengers. "Just catching my breath." Sure enough, the thug with the Klondike tooth and sawed-off showed up and took a position behind the girl.

"Drop the case," she ordered.

"Okay, I'm going to straighten up now and drop the case. After which, I'm going to put my hands up over my head." Still buying time.

"Just shut up and do it. Teddy, search him and search the case, and if you don't find it, blow his right arm off." It sounded to Charlie like girlie-girl was the boss of this operation. "Make him bleed like Randy."

He waited until "Teddy" had to look down to step over the rails without losing his balance, and that's when he sprung at her, throwing the case into her face, knocking the .38 to the ground where she would have trouble finding it in the light-and-shadow darkness, and throwing Teddy off balance. He broke into a run in the direction of the nearest and darkest shadows and tried to forget, until he was safely concealed, that his bad leg was killing him and that his gun was still in his case. He should have grabbed hers.

"Stop him, you idiot!" The girl's voice had gotten throatier, more forced. It was clear she couldn't yell very loudly without straining, and Charlie's mind raced back to a case where a felon had had his voice surgically altered for making ransom calls. He didn't want to be her kidnap victim, and he ran like hell.

The sudden, messy report of the sawed-off hit Charlie's ears just about the same time as the few pellets that grazed his left arm and leg. It echoed off the industrial buildings that lined the right-of-way, and raised a few screams from the frightened passengers. Good! They could no longer see him clearly in the shadows, and, unless they gave chase, he would soon be out of lethal range of the modified shotgun. He wagered that this was getting too messy for them. They'd search his bag. Not finding the diamond there, they'd probably make as fast an exit into the shadows as they could. Nonetheless, reaching the edges of the yards, he found the first big clump of bushes he could find, still with some leaves on them, and jumped behind them.

What he bumped into didn't feel like bushes, or the building. Then it moved. His first thought: A hobo sleeping in the bushes. Accustoming his eyes, though, he could see that he had bumped into a man in battle gear, armored vest and helmet, who was watching everything through what looked like infrared binoculars. All of this happening in split seconds, he uttered an involuntary, "What the hell?"

"Shut up, Komensky! Keep down!" came a loud whisper.

He recognized the voice immediately. It belonged to his old friend Douglas Christie. They had been through the Chicago Police Academy together and remained friends, albeit friends that didn't see each other very often, ever since. Doug's wife, Agatha, was a good forensic accountant and had helped on many a case, the last being the one on which Charlie has sustained his bad leg. Charlie whispered, "Okay, more precisely, what the hell are you doing here?"

"Apparently, I'm saving your ass. Shh! They're coming."

Charlie continued the whispered conversation. Referring to an infection that Christie had suffered after a gunshot wound, he said, "Last I heard, you had gotten some nasty clap, and it had chewed off your man parts and started on your leg."

"Very funny. Actually, my man parts are just fine, thanks. My legs a little game, though. A bit like yours."

"Fine pair to be up against three kidnappers," mumbled Charlie. "How'd you know my ass was in trouble?"

"Don't have much time. So, short version: Got on disability after rehab and this is not—I repeat, NOT!—a CPD operation. This is Homeland Security. I'm a free agent now, like you, but I contract out. We got a tip from a railfan who was up on Roosevelt Road taking pics that there were some unusual people running around the yards. When we found out the manifest had your name on it, I figured somebody's bullet did, too." Then he spoke into a communications device that had a speaker hanging down from the side of his helmet. "Alpha, two of them are near me. Subject Charlie is safe. Do you have three?"

Charlie couldn't hear the response, but Doug turned to him with a thumbs up. A shot came from somewhere on the bridge, then another. Charlie did hear the cries of pain of both the sexy moll and the dental patient as their weapons were shot out of their hands. With some luck, a few broken fingers, too. Two more shots brought them down, but, knowing federal tactics, wouldn't kill them. Questioning would be thorough and harsh. Doug said to his communicator, "Three is just rounding the back of the rail car. Do you have him, Alpha?" Two more shots. In seconds, fifty men dressed approximately like Christie swarmed the tracks.

"Don't you have to go secure the perimeter or something?"

Doug looked at Charlie. "Nope. My job's going to be easier." He quickly pulled Charlie up, and, before Charlie knew it, the handcuffs were biting into Charlie's wrists.

(ELK GROVE VILLAGE, ILLINOIS, WEDNESDAY, OCTOBER 10, 11:24PM CDT)

"Hell of a Wednesday night," Charlie thought over and over again between interrogations. He knew police procedure and intellectually knew that there would have been no way for Doug to help him escape the hours of interrogation, but all of that hadn't sunk in yet when he found himself in the back of a black SUV on the way to an unmarked warehouse in an industrial park in Elk Grove. Doug had done him the only favor he could, and that had been to just take his wallet and otherwise confirm that Charlie had been frisked, even though he hadn't. The risk to Doug, as an independent contractor, would be loss of government contracts and a slap on the wrist. But Charlie and Doug went way back, and Charlie knew that Doug would have done more if it would have done any good. Charlie's lament about a bad Wednesday had more to do with the fact that he would not get to visit with jeweler Nate Steinmetz that evening than with any discomfort. In fact the worst discomfort was the bare interrogation room, which had not even been blessed by the application of acoustic tile to the unfinished drywall. The smell of mildew and wet chipboard were at times overpowering. The HS people hadn't even bothered to install ceilings, just chicken wire mesh spread over from wall partition to wall partition, so that Charlie could see the high, metal ceiling and the bare industrial lighting a good forty feet above him. A camera peered down at him from above the mesh. He assumed that the wire had been duly attached to a high-voltage fence controller, but had no need to tamper with the camera, or to escape.

The facts that none of the interrogations had been particularly grueling, that his wallet had been given back to him, and that he still had the diamond in his pants pocket seemed encouraging. His story, as much of it as he had cared to share went along the lines of assuming that the four assailants worked for the same person who had hired Ramunda. He didn't lie when he said that nobody in New Mexico had passed any evidence along to him, but did lie several times when he was repeatedly asked whether he knew what the perpetrators—who were fast becoming known as the Four and a Half Gang—were looking for. He'd made the mistake of leaving his watch on the train, so he only guessed that he had been there about four hours when Doug Christie came in.

"We're going to be taking you to a safe house," were Doug's first words.

"Do we have to? I feel pretty safe right here."

As Charlie spoke, he noticed that Doug had briefly positioned himself to block the view of the camera. In the police academy, he and Doug had developed a working sign language. Only understood by the two of them, it worked for situations where only visual communication was possible. It involved very imperceptible movements and common tics that looked like normal quirks, a little like a catcher signaling a pitcher, but more subtle. Nothing like SWAT team hand signals. As he was still able to put his hands onto the table, even in the cuffs, with a few finger motions and wrinkling his nose, he asked if the pigs knew how to write. Doug shook his head with a simple no, which meant he had not shared the code with his employers.

Next, he asked, in code, if the pigs know how to drive? Another no told Charlie that Doug would be driving him to the safe house. Ears? Negative, they would talk more in the car. Doug had given him the opportunity to discuss the case openly and on camera. Charlie appreciated that, but he considered that he may want to visit New Mexico again, and didn't want any warrants out on him for tampering. He had yet to figure out how he was going to get around the whole debacle, now that the chance to secretly get information and then return to New Mexico appeared to be lost.

They were on the road for twenty minutes when Charlie finally decided that Doug wasn't going to initiate the conversation. The feds had watched Doug put him into the back of the black, late-model Chevy Impala, and had signed off on some kind of paperwork. The handcuffs still bit into his wrist. "Is this your Chevy?" Charlie began.

"And the bank's." Doug wasn't going to make this easy, which was his way when he felt his good nature being abused.

"You want to know what's going on, don't you?"

"That'd be nice. Seeing as I just saved your ass."

"Tell me where we're going and I'll tell you everything before we get there."

Doug Christie just looked back at Charlie through the rearview mirror and drove on for a few minutes. They were now on Itasca Road, and going south. Finally he said, "My contract includes providing a safe house for low risk persons of interest. They consider you one. I'm not sure what I think at this time, but it's up to you. We can go to a safe house and spend a week or two playing penny ante with a short deck, or you can tell me what you have that's so important, and we can go home to Aggie and a nice home-cooked dinner."

Considering the options, Charlie knew he'd have to trust Doug and started talking. He filled in details of the tiff with Linda that he'd left out, and the odd characters he'd been dealing with in New Mexico. He explained why he thought that the stone in his pants pocket was important, and why he didn't want the New Mexico authorities to get their hands on it. He also filled in the calls he had made, and revealed the contacts he had queried. "That's it."

"Are you sure you're not leaving out anything?"

He had left out the almost affair with Bernice. Or, maybe, it was the beginning of one. After all, naked bodies had been displayed. But Doug would have to tell Aggie, and then Linda would certainly hear about it, and he still loved Linda despite letting his libido get inside his head. "Nothing else to know." He disliked lying to Doug.

"Then let's get that dinner."

CHAPTER SIX

(CHICAGO, THURSDAY, OCTOBER 11, 8:33 A.M. CDT)

The next morning dawned cold and heavy. Chicago could have glorious October days with crisp, dry air and light winds, but this wasn't one of them. The Cubs had had a bad season and wouldn't be in the playoffs. The low ceiling of clouds touched the top of the Wrigley scoreboard like a bad omen. The board was one of the things that Doug could see from his back yard any day of the week. He could also have seen the downtown skyline, if it had not been for the clouds and the cold mist that filled the air and the bones of any living creature within ten city blocks of Lake Michigan.

Doug and Charlie got in the Chevy to drive to the Jeweler's Building at half past seven; this time with Charlie in the front seat and no handcuffs. What was left of his roll case Doug thoughtfully brought home in the trunk, and Charlie had managed to salvage a clean pair of Dockers and a fresh green sport shirt. The shower that morning in Doug's remodeled bathroom had felt measurably better than the one he'd had in the cheap, low-water-pressure hotel in Albuquerque. Although the Southwest Chief offered showers, Charlie had never attempted one on board, and wasn't planning to anytime soon.

The plan was for Doug to drop Charlie off and then go to police headquarters, where he would call in a few favors from a police analyst or two and run backgrounds on all of the characters. Charlie told him to hold nothing back, including the eccentric Sam Speeno. He even wanted a background on Bernie Schrader, because something deep in his bones told him the mole was in one of the police departments. Doug didn't like the plan, and Charlie had to admit there was some risk that whoever had come for him on an intercity passenger train may be staking out jewelers. But there were so, so many jewelers in Chicago, and the Jewelers Building offered unique ways for them to stay secure—at least the building Charlie had in mind.

So Charlie found himself walking from Wacker Drive to the corner of Randolph and Wabash. The fine mist in the air had become just damp enough to equate to a light drizzle, and the temperature seemed to threaten frost, though the flashing thermometer on a bank building said 52°. Doug had dropped Charlie off in front of the 1927 Jewelers Building, a middling Gothic Noveau structure that stole the name from the building where Charlie was going. Adler and Sullivan had designed the other Jewelers building, circa 1881, at 15 South Wabash. Despite the elaborate arrangements to protect jewelers and diamond merchants in the newer building, they didn't hold a candle, in Charlie's opinion, to the building that had housed the city's first community of diamond experts at the end of the 19th century.

As he looked up at Sullivan's signature cast iron façade, the deafening rumble of a Chicago 'L' made him turn and watch the four-car train make its way over the east leg of the famous Loop. It made him long for a day off when he could get downtown early in the morning and grab a seat where he could look out the front window and ride the 'L' until supper time. He hadn't had one of those in far too many years.

He liked the elevators in the old building, too. Though renovated, the two cars had retained the old grilles from the original elevators, and afforded their riders a look at the sides of the shaft moving past the cars as they rose and fell from a double sub-basement to the fifth floor. Charlie thoroughly enjoyed the ride to Steinmetz & Sons on the fourth floor, in fact finding old elevators almost as intriguing as old steam locomotives.

Here's where the real fun began. Stepping off the elevator, he walked toward what appeared to be a plate glass window. Gold leaf lettering identified the company.

STEINMETZ & SONS

DIAMONDS AND STONES OF FINE QUALITY

Through the show window, Charlie could see what appeared to be the entire showroom, empty and unattended, with all trays and cases completely devoid of any hint of merchandise whatsoever. This same apparent lack of business seemed to plague other stores on the same floor, with other showrooms equally devoid of customers or merchandise. But Charlie knew what others didn't: The architects, on the insistence of the old diamond merchants, had designed a unique and almost impenetrable security system.

Somebody looking for a way to burglarize or rob the tenants of the building might start by getting the blueprints by whatever means possible. They would show the would-be criminal exactly what Charlie was looking at now: Each showroom suite consisted of a salesroom with two large offices at the back and four small ones along one side, either left or right. Each would share a common wall with either a neighboring suite or the elevator shaft, which appeared to occupy one end of the building, but was actually located in almost the exact middle of the floor plan. This would be the key to figuring out the illusion, but the criminal would often be deterred long before that.

In fact, the showrooms that Charlie was looking at on this floor were an elaborate optical illusion created by optics, mirrors, and a slab of thick, borosilicate glass layered behind the supposedly normal plate. Done in a most ingenious fashion using a quarter scale replica of the actual showrooms, the illusion even included the images of people working in the actual offices—not the replicas—that were the one single detail that convinced the criminal that there would be nothing to steal.

To get in to see Nate Steinmetz, Charlie would now pass through the second 19th-century security device: The triple-lock entry.

Whereas a common double-lock entry involved a set of exterior doors and interior doors with an intermediate "air lock" in which a potential customer or thief could be admitted or imprisoned in the lock using automatic, electric bolts on the doors, the triple-lock device gave the jeweler or merchant the opportunity to watch the criminal "show himself." In the old days, they had used a speaking tube that adequately transmitted voices from the interior of the suite, but these had been modernized to ordinary doorbell intercoms. The ignorant thief would ring and get himself admitted to the first air lock, and see the second set of locked doors in front of him, which corresponded to his expectations from looking through the plate glass. (In fact, the air lock area was always concealed by showcases in the replicas.) Expecting to be let into the showroom, a thief would present himself as a normal customer, trying not to reveal any weapons or tools he was carrying. However, he would be prepared to draw those weapons almost simultaneously upon the merchant accepting him as a customer and passing him through the second doorway.

Charlie got himself buzzed into the air lock and stood there, facing the faux door, knowing it was not real. The protocol involved standing in this way, because only genuine walk-in customers or potential hold up men, would not know that the real door would open to his right—maybe to his left in another sales suite—where a thief might become confused and "show himself" too soon while still confined to the confusing set of three doors, one false door, and two air locks! Charlie read the sign on the faux door, which he knew had been composed by Nate Steinmetz, himself.

THIS STORE IS NOT A GUN FREE ZONE.
WE ARE WELL ARMED.

GONIFS ENTER AT YOUR OWN RISK.

PRESS BUTTON AT LEFT TO BE ALLOWED IN.

WARNING! YOU MAY BE SHOT ON SIGHT.

The button was an old fashioned doorbell button that looked like it belonged on a Victorian house. He chuckled and followed directions. The wall panel to his right opened up and he stepped into the second air lock, where a window set at eye level and made of a heavy sheet of bulletproof Lexan allowed communication with Nate's clerk through an equally bulletproof lazy Susan similar to the ones used in gas stations in really, really bad neighborhoods. Through the window, he saw Nate coming out of his office to meet him.

Charlie knew Nate was Jewish, and so did most of Nate's customers. Neither Charlie nor the customers could tell just how Jewish. Whether for business, or as the result of a grotesque sense of humor, he Nate acted as though he were the quintessential, New York Jew. Far from Hasidic, he nonetheless wore a full beard long enough to cover his shirt collar and the knot of his outdated tie. He was short, a good foot shorter than Charlie, with a round, jovial face and bright eyes that looked happy most of the time. His visage could cloud up; the eyes could pierce you like a knife if he took offense or chose to expose real or imagined stupidity. In the vernacular of his Jewishness, his own practical common sense could not be criticized.

Today, Nate's suit was a light brown, outdated style that suggested he got his clothes somewhere in a secondhand store. He wore black, plastic-rimmed glasses and an old, felt Borsalino, black with a brown band, that was a size small for him. A string of unraveled brown thread from the band hung about an inch off one side of the battered brim, as though a repair was coming undone. Scuffed, brown oxford shoes that looked like they had been dispensed by Florsheim in the mid-sixties completed the outfit. Despite their age, a sales tag of some sort still dangled and flapped from one shoelace.

When Charlie had gotten the last of the bolted doors closed behind him, Nate shook his hand and embraced him warmly. "Come, let me look at you," he said while smiling and holding Charlie at arm's length like he was examining a large stuffed toy. "Stop looking at the floor and face me so I can see in your eyes. God be praised, you look healthy." This discouraged his visitors from talking too much about their health, and Charlie knew it.

"Yeah, Nate. Happy and healthy, except for this damn gimp of mine."

"Chicken soup." Nate smiled again and conducted Charlie into his office with his right index finger up in the air as though he were testing the wind. He said nothing more about soup, as if it needed no other explanation.

When they had settled into his office, Nate behind the desk in a worn leather executive chair and Charlie in a wool-upholstered Queen Anne chair that had seen better days, the latter looked around. The entire room was painted a light brown with gold trim. It looked like a remodel from the 70s. The window to Nate's left looked out over an alley, and the magenta drapes that hung awkwardly on a bent rod seemed to be stiff with dust. On the wall to Nate's right were hundreds of family photographs, some in frames and some simply stapled to the plaster. In some, Nate seemed to be dining with celebrities, including the late Sammy Davis, Jr. In others, he was standing with men, women and children, all bearing some resemblance to him and certainly to his wife. The wedding photo was proudly displayed in the center of the array. In yet another, a young Nate Steinmetz dressed in an Israeli military uniform stood with a dozen other similarly clad men over a sign that said IDF Heil and another word that the photographer had let get out of focus. In still another, Steinmetz wore a cap and gown and held a diploma with about a hundred other graduates of Vienna Academy.

A small window looked out onto the showroom, and Charlie remembered that it was a one-way mirror. Large, finished wood cabinets occupied both corners opposite Nate's desk. The wall behind Nate held two big paintings: one of Ronald Reagan as President, and the other of Reagan as a cowboy. These were new. Charlie thought he recalled a single large painting of Golda Meir. Nate saw him looking and said, "Shows that anybody can be a politician, but few politicians can be cowboys. So is Charlie Komensky—God forbid I still think he should be a good Jewish boy from the north side—buying or selling today?

"Maybe half Jewish on my mother's side but baptized Catholic," said Charlie, but he thought, "Odd that Sam Speeno asked me the same thing!" He pulled the diamond out of his pocket and held it out to Nate, whose eyes turned big and round as half dollars.

Then a wide grin lit Steinmetz up like the eighth day of Hanukkah. "Oh, selling!"

"Neither. I just want to find out what you can tell me about that stone."

Looking disappointed, Nate took out a jeweler's loupe and squinted at the dazzling rock for a full minute. Then he got up suddenly and ran to the door where they had entered. Looking furtively out into the showroom and then back into it, he turned the bolt. "I'd pull the drapes, but as you can see, there's nothing but a brick wall on the other side of the alley." He sat down heavily and examined the stone through the loupe again. "Shame you're not Jewish. If you were Jewish, you would want information and sell the stone both. I'd give you such a deal."

"So there's a story?"

"Big one. Let me get my *microptica* first." Getting up again, he ran to one of the cases, which he opened. A large gemologist's microscope emerged on a sliding platform as the cabinet doors swung away. Placing the stone at the objective end, Nate oofed and grunted until he got the focus right, then mumbled a few things, ran back to his desk to write down a number, and then went back to get the stone. The cabinet closed with a thump as the spring-loaded platform slid back in. Before Charlie knew it, Nate put the stone onto a small, velvet covered pallet of the kind he used to display gems in his showroom, placed the pallet and stone on his desk, and sat back as if admiring it.

"Look at that sparkle, Mister Charles Komensky, and tell me that it doesn't make you feel all warm inside that you have in your presence one of the truly magnificent creations of Jehovah, God of Jacob, God of Isaac, King David be blessed. How did you come by this blessing?"

Charlie squinted at the diamond merchant. "I'm not fooled by all this god of blah, blah crap, Nate. I've known you long enough to see the little wheels turning under that old hat of yours. When did you steal that hat from your grandfather again?"

Bowing his head sideways, Nate acquiesced. "I understand, you must have the story first. But know this, Komensky! We who possess this lovely item are in grave danger. Just so you should know if I don't get to finish the story."

"There is no we. But go on."

"Just in case you have never heard of it, there is, located in Antwerp Belgium, something called the Antwerp Diamond Center. Inside this magnificent structure—not as magnificent as this one, but close—there are 160 underground vaults that are used to hold diamonds. If you are in possession of a diamond of any value beyond being a bauble that poor men pay for at great interest so they may engage themselves to be married, chances are that it has passed through the Antwerp Diamond Center between the mine and the merchant. Stones of traders of many companies are there because of the enhanced security. But those belonging to and cut by Antwerp merchants are particularly identifiable because of a unique cut that includes a laser code not known to any but the most honest of merchants."

"I know about laser marks," interrupted Charlie. "And you're going to lie one way or the other if you tell me that you know the code." He laughed, but he could already see where the story was going.

Again Nate bowed his head to one side. "In I think it was 2003, 123 of the 160 vaults were emptied by diamond thieves. Over $100 million worth of stones was the announced take, but I think that was just the insured amount. Police and others who know the diamond business thought it was more like upwards of $500 million.

"The scoundrels who deprived the world of all these beautiful stones were a group of burglars known inside criminal circles as the School of Turin, as in Italy. Everybody who is anybody in the business, however, knows that these are just a highly organized group of mercenaries who were being paid for a good night's work. The alleged planner and inside man was fingered as an Italian businessman and sometime trader with connections to the Sicilians. His name is Leonardo Notarbartolo.

"Now, Charles, I don't know that I believe for one minute that he was the man responsible for this, although a scapegoat was needed at the time. The man or woman responsible had to be on the inside, and Notarbartolo was convicted on grossly circumstantial evidence. He did eight of ten, a good percentage, and is now . . .." Steinmetz threw up his hands. "God knows where!

"The diamonds have never been recovered. Unless…"

The diamond on the desk seemed to sparkle at Charlie, as though it were trying to speak to him. "They're starting to surface?"

Nate winked. "This is definitely one of the Antwerp diamonds. The little sparkler would buy you a nice BMW. So tell me how you happen to have it in your pocket, and I'll tell you what else I know."

His story wasn't as interesting as Nate's, except for the part about the stone probably being a warning shot between two criminal groups, a shot that Charlie had personally deflected. Although a hustler, Nate had Charlie's trust, as did some of his colleagues on and off the force, so he held back little.

"What is it about New Mexico?" Nate asked. The question was so off the wall that Charlie didn't know how to answer. His puzzled look made Nate explain. "Word is that a tribe of Indians out there want to liquidate a collection that includes a number of precious stones, some diamonds. I never heard why, but it would be interesting if some of them were from Antwerp."

"I don't know about that. But is that all?" Charlie was thinking, "Why did he drop that bomb?"

Nate shook his head. "No, that's just a factoid. What I really know is this: There have been periodic rumblings that maybe better than three quarters of the Antwerp diamonds were moved to the United States, maybe through the port of Long Beach. Those rumblings have come along with queries about moving the stones to buyers now that the heat has cooled down and before Notarbartolo surfaces. Sicilians are behind the rumblings, but other names I do not know. You and I both know who would. And the Cosa Nostra is not bashful about thinning the herd when it's time for a payoff."

"Testa?"

"You dare say his name, not I. I was merely venturing an opinion." Nate Steinmetz stood up as if he were going to be evicted from his office. His voice became more urgent. "If you're not going to let me buy that and cut it up so that by tonight there will be no identification, then you should take it before it gets me in trouble. I am only human, and being poisoned by something like boiler wash may be bad for my youthful complexion." He held out a hand to Charlie. "Good luck, my friend. God be with you."

"Don't forget shot. The dead lawyer was shot," Charlie pointed out as he shook hands and left. He was out on Randolph Street before he had organized his thoughts, and the weather hadn't gotten any better. A call to Doug revealed that, as with most deep backgrounds, none of the players were clean and sanitary. He asked Doug to pick him up in about an hour on Michigan Avenue, because he was going to take a long, cold walk in Millennium Park to jar his brain into developing some kind of theory. In the meantime, he suggested that Doug put out the word that he wanted to talk to somebody in the outfit, somebody with Sicilian ties. Those persons disenchanted with "the life" or inclined to lean on both sides of the fence would jump on it.

CHAPTER SEVEN

(RIVERSIDE, ILLINOIS, THURSDAY, OCTOBER 11, 3:45PM
CDT)

Doug took Charlie home that afternoon. The park had been shrouded in mist and fog from Lake Michigan, and the only other people walking in that weather had been pickpockets and armed muggers. After witnessing an attempted mugging and chasing the mugger away by drawing his gun, Charlie had returned to Michigan Avenue and just waited for Doug on a bus bench. At home, his mind wasn't any clearer than it had been when he'd left Nate's, and he knew why. He'd absent-mindedly been speed-dialing her number from his cell phone; he didn't know how many times. He couldn't get Linda out from under the edges.

Linda Chelwood occupied a brick bungalow in Riverside, which had been an affluent suburb of Chicago since creation. When he had been working on the Berwyn P.D., her house had been only a quarter mile from headquarters. Nonetheless, he'd only been inside once, but that had been for a three day stay after he'd had a second surgery on his bum leg. Any other time, he'd always met her in Oak Brook or somewhere else where they'd planned a date. Though he'd never criticized it in her presence, the house seemed too big for her. It really looked like a bungalow on steroids, and the fact that many of the original wood-frame windows had been replaced back in the 50s with glass block didn't do anything to discourage that appearance. Like many of the houses in Riverside, the front rested close to the street, so that it had an extraordinarily large backyard, with two apple trees and a water garden complete with windmills and a water wheel. Again, he'd only been allowed into the back yard once. His suggestion that she put in a backyard scale model garden railroad was probably the reason.

He arrived with no plan. He knew this was likely his first mistake, but he also knew himself well enough to know he would not be able to concentrate on the case until he got this whole thing out of his system. He knew he'd done the wrong thing with their trip and treating Linda as a hired hand when they were supposed to be on a romantic vacation. Parking his Taurus on the street—the same Taurus that had been fished out of an Iowa ditch two summers before—he immediately noticed the car in Linda's side driveway that wasn't hers. She had good taste in cars, but she was frugal, at least, and the Toyota Avalon looked expensive. Unfortunately for his imagination, now running full tilt toward a baseless conclusion, her old Lincoln Town Car was there, too. Linda was just too classy a lady to step out on him without letting him know to his face that the engagement was off, but this whole situation was off. "I'm not being ridiculous," he told himself. This was no different from his cop mindset of trusting almost nobody and suspecting that every circumstance and every chance encounter needed to be parsed to find the clue.

In this case, he couldn't help himself and called Doug to run the plate on the strange sedan. "You and I are running out of favors over at HQ," Doug reacted.

"I think we should run it." Once Charlie had made up his mind, Doug had never been able to talk him out of anything.

Doug hesitated. "Wait. Aggie says she knows that car." There was a pause. "That's Spencer Dinelli's car." Dinelli was another accountant who worked both forensic and business. Charlie felt a little relief. Although Spencer had been known to do some work on the dark side, he had helped Linda out of a tax jam a few years back. It was probably business. "You okay?"

"Yeah. I guess I'd better not interrupt," he told Doug, knowing full well that he wanted to. What he was really telling himself was that he didn't want to find out what would happen if he called her or rang the front doorbell. Spencer was a looker and a good dresser, six pack abs, probably shaved his balls just in case they fell out at the gym, and more in Linda's financial ballpark. Charlie's finances were more like across the street from the ballpark in the cheap parking lot where you can't get your car out until everyone else moves. She might tell him to go to hell either way, and the thought paralyzed him. "I'll talk to you later," said Charlie, hitting "end call" and putting the cell phone back on the seat of the Taurus.

Struggling mightily, he lingered, hoping the owner of the Avalon would leave before he had to consider himself an obsessed boyfriend, but it didn't happen. It gave him an idea, though. What if the murder and the thing with the diamond was all about accounting? If the outfit was just thinning the herd in preparation for putting the stones on the market, as Nate had suggested, why would you want to warn your next victim? And if, as he'd originally thought, it was revenge with a message, then why go to so much trouble to get the diamond back from him? On the other hand, maybe it had been fully expected that the diamond would return to the fold after the murder. And it would, if the "fold" were the original owner, which was Antwerp, and somebody there was signaling they were about to murder all of the original burglars unless they sent back the diamonds. The police would eventually have to "account" for the evidence by giving it back to the rightful owner.

His new theory fascinated him, and he sat there in the Taurus playing with the alternate realities that would make the whole scenario fit together into a valid motive for corporate murder. He really didn't want to leave Linda's place, anyway, and this just gave him an excuse.

He had just about put all the pieces together in his mind, but in reality had simply fallen asleep in the car and started dreaming about the case. In spite of it being only late afternoon, the ordeal of the past couple of days had caught up with him.

He jumped at the noise of a tap on the window. "Huh? Sorry officer, I was just," he said before he shook off the nap. But the face at the passenger side window wasn't that of a police officer. The man who stood outside his car was short, stocky, and wearing a brown leather jacket and a polyester knit golf hat over wool worsted dress slacks. He had a mushy face, showing both signs of a good appetite and excessive drinking, and a pugilist's nose. Charlie made him to be about the same age as himself, and he had a vague feeling he had seen the guy somewhere before. He couldn't see the man's shoes, but knew they'd be expensive. So would the silk socks and the gun that the man had slung in the bulge of a shoulder holster under his left arm. The man was clean shaven, the kind of shave you see on actors and on men who have enough money and leisure time to see the barber every afternoon and go over the *Racing News* in detail while waiting their turn.

Charlie rolled down the passenger side window with difficulty—it hadn't worked right since the car had been dried out. The man put his left hand on the top of the car and leaned in. "You Charlie Komensky?" he asked with a broad smile.

The man wasn't menacing, but Charlie knew how to play the game. "Who wants to know?"

"A person with mutual interests."

"If our interests are mutual, then you already know who I am; and you probably been following me since I got home."

"Fair enough, Charlie."

Before he could say anything else, Charlie corrected him. "Only my dearest friends call me that. Are you one of my dearest friends?"

"Fair enough, Mr. Komensky. You ain't one of those ex-cop pee-eyes that have an itchy trigger finger, are ya?"

"What if I am."

"'Cause I was just about to unzip my jacket and get out a document that I'm supposed to deliver to you, an' I wouldn' want you to think I was actin' in an aggressive manner." He followed through and pulled a business card out of an inside jacket pocket. "My name's Georgio, by the way. Here."

Charlie took the smooth, white card. The back was blank, except for a small symbol that Charlie didn't recognize. Printed in black in one corner, so small that it might have gone unnoticed, it struck Charlie that it might have been a microscopic rendering of a coat of arms. The front of the card was also printed in black, simple sans serif lettering. Only an address and business appeared, not Georgio's name, and not anyone else.

Entrepreneurial Enterprises

3648 South Jasper Place

Chicago, Illinois 60609

"Yeah," thought Charlie, smiling as he read it. "Criminal entrepreneurial enterprises." He checked again, just to see if the small mark on the back was any criminal symbol he recognized. The business card was the mildest form of invitation that one could get from a crime family, whether it was Mafia, Tong, Shamrock or Russkaya; more than mild would have been anything from a bag over the head to kidnapping family.

Georgio also smiled. "I see we understand each other." Perhaps the strongest expression of mutual respect one could get from the mob. Charlie was on a roll. "But just to cement the relationship, you might want to know that I'm not the only one who's been following you since you left home." He cocked his head in a direction diagonal and across the street. There, barely concealed around the corner of a big house, a shadowy figure, androgynous in a long dark coat and a wide-brimmed hat, lurked in a manner indicating some experience in surveillance. Charlie hadn't known he had been followed by either tail. "I think it's a woman, late thirty, early forty, an' her car's down the street. A black Mercedes. If it makes any difference, I don't think she knows we made her."

"Yeah," Charlie smiled again. "It makes a difference."

Georgio stood up, then leaned down into the car window again. "An' just so you can tell the boss that I told you: The info is for your personal use, an' lose the tail before you show up at that address."

"Got it. Eyes only, and lose the tail."

Georgio nodded, stood up, and started walking south down Riverside Drive. Knowing it would do him no good to tail the tail, especially with another rear end appendage on his trail, Charlie just sat and watched until Georgio walked around the next corner. Some detective, he'd missed two people tailing him in one day. If there was a road test for private dick, he'd flunked it.

Looking back, he saw the female tail still standing at the corner of the big, Victorian house. Damn! He should have asked Georgio whether she could have done anything to his car while he slept. Was Georgio paying attention? Surely, if his boss wanted to see Charlie, then Georgio would not leave him in the predicament of having his car tampered with. In any case, he'd have to keep an eye out. Protocol would dictate that he not show up on Jasper Place, wherever that was, too soon. A prompt appearance would suggest urgent interest rather than courteous deference to authority, and would also make Georgio's boss wary that Charlie hadn't taken enough care in getting rid of the shadow. Then, too, showing up quickly wouldn't allow Charlie enough time to arrange for backup, and the boss probably knew that.

Charlie decided that he'd go home first, take a shower, try to call Linda one last time—or six—and then decide if his meeting would be that night or the next day. He would also then have time to check in with Doug, who he considered his "Linda" for research purposes and for keeping him in tune with Chicago Police. He opened the driver's door so he could be ready to roll out and run if he heard anything unusual when turning on the ignition. Most car bombs were placed under the hood or under the gas tank at the rear of the vehicle. You could escape them if you were prepared, vigilant rather than unsuspecting. "Here goes nothing." He turned the ignition key.

Nothing happened, except the engine turned over, and he made a point of leaving rubber from his mostly bald tires as he pulled from the curb and made a U-turn on Riverside. A logical move to test his tail, he drove into the business district to hit an ATM for some cash. While at the ATM, he checked and rechecked for any sign of his tail, made sure he kept the printout in case he needed to have Doug get a warrant for the security video later, and pulled forward, again waiting a good minute before driving off. Either she was good—real good—or they were actually staking out Linda's place and there was another tail on him, one Georgio hadn't told him about. Either way, he detected nothing and decided it was safe to head for home. He got no further than three blocks before getting stopped by the flashing lights and dropping gates at a railroad crossing.

Charlie had taken the same route so often that he was a little surprised by getting stopped at that time of day. The freights on this line were usually long and slow, and not dispatched through the neighborhoods during rush hour. Each municipality has its own ordinances about blocked crossings, and fines could mount up. Oh, well. It would give him time to consider his surroundings and keep another eye out for the tail. He also knew deep down that he would enjoy doing a little train watching.

He was in the right lane of two going north, and there were businesses on both sides of the street behind him. Parked cars lined both curbs, and none of them seemed to be occupied. In these older neighborhoods, none of the businesses had any off-street parking to speak of. Next to him at the gate was an older model, maroon Mercury with an elderly couple. Not likely they were following him. An old, red Dodge pickup with a chrome bumper that had seen better days was just pulling up behind him, but it stopped at a respectable distance and didn't seem to pose a threat. Because of its high stance, Charlie couldn't see its driver. The pedestrians, now standing and waiting or running across the double track before the train got there, also seemed unthreatening and uninterested in him.

The three-chime horn from a diesel locomotive cut the air, but from some distance away. Blaring the standard warning for an American grade crossing, used wherever modern noise ordinances and fancy gate protection didn't eliminate the use of locomotive horns altogether, the approaching train was giving a warning for the first of several urban crossings to the east. Braaaaaap. Braaaaaap. Brap. Braaaaaap. This would continue for each of the other three crossings Charlie knew to be east of where he was sitting. Because the right of way was narrow, Charlie couldn't see the approaching locomotive from his car. Then he heard a horn from the opposite direction giving the same signal. It wasn't an echo. Two trains would probably meet at the crossing and pass, but the westbound train would be slowing. He knew this, because he knew the layout of the tracks on this line; and two tracks became one no more than a half mile west of the crossing.

Now he knew he was going to be delayed there for some time, as the eastbound train would be going no faster than he had expected the westbound train to be going. He knew he was thinking paranoid, but paranoid or not, he asked himself, "Could somebody who wanted the diamond he was carrying manipulate the train dispatching?" Dismissing it as just too far-fetched, he still took a good look around to see where he was vulnerable. The chance to make a U-turn and get out of the traffic had long since passed, so he decided to stay and wait.

As he expected, the first red and white locomotive passed on the far track moving east. It couldn't have been going more than fifteen miles an hour. Empty auto rack cars followed the engine before the final Braaap! from the westbound train was followed by its slightly dirtier, but still red and white, locomotive, rumbling into the crossing at not more than ten miles an hour and slowing. A second locomotive, not quite as dirty as the first, followed; and on the rear platform of the second locomotive Charlie saw another shadowy figure. How paranoid! He couldn't convince himself that this wasn't the same figure staking out Linda's place!

This was impossible! No railroad would allow it! This had to be a coincidence, a conjuring of his fatigue, being surprised by Georgio, and the frightening feeling that he was somehow losing control.

Distracted and focused on the shadowy figure as he was, the knock on his passenger side window make him jump. He had his .38 half out of the holster before he realized it came from a poorly dressed, dirty, and bearded man in an old baseball cap: apparently a homeless man taking advantage of the stopped traffic to panhandle drivers. He let go of the gun and waved the man away, but the man knocked again. Now distracted even further, and trying to get another glimpse at the second locomotive, receding ever further from the crossing even if at a crawl, he yelled an obscenity at the panhandler. Being completely out of character for him, he was sorry the second he did it, but it was too late.

The man growled at him, then pounded the roof of the Taurus with such force that Charlie was sure there would be a dent. But what really scared Charlie was when the man bent back down and flashed a toothless grin. It only lasted a fraction of a second before the man started walking toward the truck behind the Taurus, but it rattled Charlie so much that he started to ask himself if it was just part of a bigger message. But a message from whom? And how many messages were there?

(BERWYN, ILLINOIS, OCTOBER 11, 10 P.M. TO FRIDAY, OCTOBER 12, 5:30 A.M. CDT)

Getting only fitful sleep interrupted by repeated nightmares didn't make it any easier for Charlie to get up the next morning, or to get ready for his meeting with the mob functionary on Jasper Place. The whole thing with Linda, something he thought he could handle because they had been on the outs before, had started to weigh more heavily on him that night. But just before bed and just after finishing a third of a bottle of bourbon, it had dawned on him that the diamond in his pocket was so much more what Linda deserved than the hammered piece of sheet metal he had given her for an engagement ring after the Flat Tire Murders[*] had played out. It was quaint at the time; cute, as much as Charlie hated the word, and she had never chastised him for the ring in particular, but a classy lady like her deserved so much more—at least in his mind.

[*]The account of Charlie's investigation of the murders of Danny Flatwood and Seth Sharedream is told in *The Flat Tire Murders* available from Pagination Books as an eBook from Amazon for Kindle, as a paperback from CreateSpace, or from the author.

The first nightmare, if he chose to call it that, wasn't that bad really: Linda and Bernice Schrader, the buxom deputy, taunting him and making him decide who he wanted to go to bed with. He awoke in a sweat, and fell asleep to immediately fall into the same dream, which changed to where the two women were torturing him, and then he was torturing them with bloodied tools in gruesome ways that would make an axe murderer cringe. The nightmare then shifted to where they were all being held hostage by a shadowy mob figure that sat in a large chair, backlit and as if on stage risers, and with the shadowy figure from the locomotive standing by his side. All of a sudden, he recognized her face. He knew who she was. And then he woke up again and the recollection was gone. The nightmare repeated several more times in several variations of the same stories, the same scenes and people saying the same things, until in the last version, he was in the same mobster's room, the chair was empty, and the shadowy figure of the woman from the train became Linda, who was first laughing at him, then yelling at him, "Grow up and be a man! Charlie, you useless loser! You'll never figure this one out. It's a case you can't solve. And if you ever try to sleep with that woman again . . . "   The last part stayed with him after he shaved and sat down to a bowl of dry cornflakes— the milk had spoiled while he was out of town. He hadn't even gotten a chance to read the morning *Trib*, because Linda had the newsboy suspend deliveries while they were on vacation.

If Nate had been right, it wouldn't be so far-fetched to discover strong mob connections to the original diamond thieves. If so, Charlie asked himself, why send out two messengers to watch over him? If it was an internal dispute? Whatever name you put on organized crime, it had the basic structure that came from the old Italian Cosa Nostra, and it always had its little turf wars going on. Nowadays, the wars just weren't as overt. The average honest citizen who kept his nose clean and his eyes off drugs, gambling or prostitution could be confident that the wars would never touch him. At most, John Q. Public would see a few lines in one of the few newspapers still in business and chalk it up to police going after a bunch of old Europeans who would just die off if they were left alone. The honest guy would ask, "What about the youth gangs selling street drugs, the private meth labs, the online sex?" Mr. Average would never really know how much of the current structure of the old Mafia had evolved to incorporate those new forms of illegal profit, and how much time and effort—and money—they spent to keep the general public from seeing Mafiosi as anything more than just a bunch of toothless old tigers dying off in the shadows of the concrete jungle.

Whoa! Concrete jungle! Now there's a metaphor he hadn't used since he taught a few criminology classes at Morton College. He realized with some embarrassment that his students must have seen him as extraordinarily retro.

Nevertheless, he'd taught them that theft of property had always been a big part of mob business. From the merchandise that "fell off the back of a truck," to high class art, and everything in between, the pie chart of gross mob cash receipts would have a tasty wedge where property, be it by burglary or armed robbery, was concerned. To what part of the bottom line of what mob segment's ledgers would the Antwerp diamonds contribute? By the time he got into the Taurus, looked over his shoulder for a couple of times, and got out onto Twenty-Sixth Street, he had shaken off the nightmares and resolved his determination to find out—today, if possible.

CHAPTER EIGHT

In telling the story of what happened to him next, at a hastily called lunch meeting with Doug Christie, Charlie doubted his sanity. He found his hands shaking and his mouth almost too dry to speak despite multiple refills of hot coffee. He had hardly touched his burger—and that was saying something for Charlie—before beginning his story. "I don't know if I should be telling you this," he began. After choking on a piece of lettuce leaf, he looked around before continuing. Everyone at his favorite restaurant, including the waitresses with whom he was always chummy and familiar, seemed to be watching him choke. He and Doug were in his greasy spoon of choice on the west side, cleverly called Grounded Burgers; and he had never questioned the food, but now he found himself silently asking if "they" could have put something in his burger.

Doug was supposedly "on duty" and was going out of his way to be patient with Charlie. He finally said, "Look! If you're not going to tell me what you called me here for, I'm going to leave."

"Okay, okay! Here's the story: I drove out to the address on Jasper Place, the one the mob guy Georgio gave me. I assumed that I didn't have to make an appointment, and there wasn't a phone number on the card anyway. I felt pretty good after psyching myself up this morning and shaking off the bad dreams. You know what I mean, the kind that the police shrinks say are PTSD related and then they keep you coming back and sitting on the couch once a week to the end of days just so you can bare your soul and then they ask if you're sexually frustrated. I usually answer yes.

"Anyway, I had the windows rolled down and the soft rock station on and, like I said, I felt pretty good. Like this morning I was going to accomplish something. Here's this great, sunny, October Friday morning and it's the best weather ever. Chill in the air but even though, you know, we've had those no-burn ordinances on the books since you and I were rookies and before, there's the smell of burning leaves in the air. You can take a deep breath and feel like you're breathing Life. It's what it's all about, you know?"

Doug nodded his understanding and picked up an empty coffee cup to wave in front of a passing waitress. The place was a stainless steel and Formica kind of joint, and he had no trouble catching her attention for a hefty pour that overflowed and dribbled into the aisle. The waitress, a neatly trimmed brunette about 40, didn't think for a moment about wiping it up and let it form a nice splotch in the industrial-grade carpet. As usual, she was half focused on her customers and half on the HD screen closed-captioning CNN and hanging over the kitchen end of the lunch counter. "My kind of place," observed Doug to nobody in particular as he checked to make sure he didn't drip any on himself.

"Anyway," continued Charlie. Anyway seemed like the word of the day. "Anyway, I haven't been over to the old stockyards area for a long time, and it took me longer than it should have to find Jasper Place. But that's okay, too, 'cause the neighborhood around there don't smell bad like it used to.

Sure, the stockyards were gone before I was old enough to drive, but those processing plants still used to stink up the neighborhoods something terrible. I finally figured out that Jasper Place is this little street that only runs for one block between 37th Street and an industrial spur track where there used to be a sort of marshaling yard for switching operations in the area. That's when I remembered that it was the only place in the neighborhood that used to smell good, 'cause there's an old commercial bakery at the end of the street that's still working.

"So the address that I'm looking for is across the street from the bakery. Those old buildings were probably built maybe nineteen-ten or twenty and they're solid—red brick and heavy timber and four stories with fifteen-foot ceilings and basements. The address I'm looking for is the same but doesn't have a company name on it. The only parking in there is either on the street or in back along the tracks and there's lots and lots of old, empty semitrailers parked in there; weeds growing through the wheels, you know?

"Anyway, I don't see any cars parked by my address. I would have expected a couple of black ones in the fifty grand retail range, you know? Now I'm thinking this is a trap, although there's bakers across the street having a break in their white aprons and hairnets and there's a lunch wagon coming down the street. I park and consider buying a hot dog or a tamale or something, and then I realize that the lunch wagon is selling flatbread sandwiches and salads with Pellegrino and probably couldn't manage a cup o' Joe unless they ran down to Micky D's for it. Then I notice that there's a homeless guy sitting across the back alley under one of the trailers, and he's just looking at me like he lost a cigarette up my nose or something. Worse, I can't tell right away, but he looks a lot like the guy who banged on my car roof yesterday. Like I said, I can't tell right away.

"Before I know it, a semi pulls up and blocks my view of him, or maybe his of me. The driver jumps out and heads for the lunch wagon—it ain't lunch; take my word for it—so I think that I better just get going and chalk it up to 'nobody expected me to show up this soon.' Or maybe I was late. Now, these old buildings have front doors that are still glass. I can't believe that somebody hasn't just thrown a brick through it, the way the neighborhoods have deteriorated over the years; but this one is solid plate glass. So I figure it wouldn't hurt to take a closer look through the glass.

"Inside there's a staircase with worn terrazzo steps. You know the kind: they're cupped so badly that you could spill a whole cup of coffee in there and it wouldn't run down to the next step. There's a flight going up on the right and a flight going down on the left. The open door at the top of the stairs on the right says 'empty' to me. Nothing on the main floor except dusty floorboards. But stuck to the post holding the bannister in between the two flights is a card just like the one Georgio gave me. Diagonal slash of cheap scotch tape holding it up there like Georgio or somebody was in a hurry when they put it up. It wasn't faded; didn't look like it had been there a long time. So I concluded it was for my benefit and knocked as hard as I could on the glass. No answer.

Doug stopped him at this point and said, "'Long about then you should have called me. Smelled like a trap; looked like a trap. Hell, they were probably watching you on a scope from somewhere."

"Yeah. I thought of that." Charlie leaned over the table with an even more distressed look. "But now I think they were just trying to scare the shit out of me."

"Looks like they succeeded." Doug laughed a nervous laugh that normally would have irritated Charlie. When he realized that Charlie's expression had become even more serious, he said, "Oh, shit! They did, didn't they?"

"Pretty much. When I looked real hard down the steps, into the gloom of the basement, I saw what I thought was a model train layout! You know how I am with trains, even the kind you run around the Christmas tree. So I went looking for another way in; couldn't very well have broken in with all those bakers across the street munching pita and swilling Italian water. So I avoided the trailer lot where homeless guy might still be huddled under his trailer and walked around the other side of the building. When I get to the back—here's the good part—there's this old railroad siding not connected to the system anymore, and there's an old hopper car sitting there pretty as you please. This thing's got to be fifty years old if it's a day, wood slats and all, just like they used to deliver coal back in the fifties. No shit! I figure that this building used to get deliveries of coal for heating, and when they made the last one before they converted to gas, they didn't need the old car any more, either, and just left it there. Sure enough, the expiration date on the brake system is 12-53."

Doug laughed—this time a hearty, irreverent laugh of relief. "Ha! Is that all that's got you so riled up? What's there to be scared about an old railroad car? Unless there's a body in it?"

"More subtle than that. I crawl into the basement through the chute that the coal dumped through back in the old days. Sure enough, the boiler room has this big old steam boiler converted to gas, but I can still see the old stokers with the worm screws that pulled in the coal from the bin. You know I love that kind of stuff. It drew me in! But it gets worse.

"Somebody's been using the basement and using it for a pretty fancy model railroad. The rest of the basement is fixed up really nice, with curtains on the old windows and oak paneling below a chair rail. With the old window frames, it made it look like the inside of an old country railroad station. You know, I'm still being a detective, but my railroad gene is fully kicked in. I spend a little time going through the few drawers and cabinets scattered around, and I find nothing but tools. Then I can't resist any more, and I find the light switch.

"Damn! This model train layout isn't just a four by eight. This thing is big! It's a desert theme with a double track main line all the way around and a full fourteen track yard and a Spanish mission style station I think looks like the station in Albuquerque. The yard is packed with freight cars, and there's an engine terminal, too, with a ten-stall roundhouse and some pretty expensive brass model steam locomotives parked in there. So I'm walking around this huge layout and I notice that there's also a narrow gauge section: a little track coming down off of a mountainside, and a little old station and terminal with a coaling tower and water standpipe for watering the miniature locomotives—what people who aren't really into model railroads would call 'cute.'" There was that word again, cute. He visibly cringed as if in pain.

Doug saw the reaction, and started to say something, but Charlie held up a hand to stop him and went on, "I'm about to start strolling around some more—you know that I can spend hours with a model railroad—and I realize that there's something familiar about the little narrow gauge engine terminal. My heart skips a beat when I see this little locomotive with its front end poking out of the model engine house, one just like the engine house up in Taos County."

Discussions about trains turned an off switch on Doug's brains, even model trains run by mob kingpins; but this last thing switched them back on. "You're shittin' me."

"Not just that! I mean . . . I'm not shittin' you . . . but here's the smokebox door open on the locomotive, and right in front of the pilot—cowcatcher to you—is a small, soot smudged model corpse in a cheap lawyer suit with four model figures, two deputies, an exotic medical examiner, and yours truly standing around it!"

Doug didn't say anything, but just looked at Charlie in disbelief. Charlie saw it as either surprise or Doug thought he was around the bend. "You're probably thinking that this isn't something for me to be in shock over, and you'd be right, if there wasn't more.

"To start with, I saw this as more of a warning to stay out of mob business than as an admission of guilt, but now I'm not so sure. I think there's good warnings and helpful warnings and then there's bad warnings. I've been getting a bad feeling out of this case right along. So it would have taken more than this to derail me. And yeah, I know I just made a bad pun."

"You just have a bad feeling because you love trains so much and don't like to think they can be used as murder weapons."

Charlie shook his head. "In this case, not weapons for murder, but the backdrop, and maybe for that and something worse."

"What's worse than murder?"

"Serial murder." He held up a hand when Doug started to protest that this wasn't a serial murder. "Hear me out. I think you'll agree when I show you the rest of it." He got up and, without explaining why, went out into the foyer of the restaurant where they kept the newspaper machines and the stacks of free real estate listings and neighborhood *Penny Saver* papers. Doug knew better than to yell after him, and when he came back, he threw the copy of the Trib he had purchased onto the table, just missing Doug's half-empty coffee cup. "Look in the Chicagoland section."

The editors of the venerable newspaper, now read by fewer than half of the potential news readers in the city because of the inroads of electronic media, usually reserved the Chicagoland section for special interest articles of local color, and for hard news on occurrences that wouldn't necessarily get a national audience. Translate that as those that wouldn't get much play on the wire services unless they were of the variety defined by anything from kittens rescued from trees by service dogs to felons so stupid as to convict themselves right at the scene of the crime.

In the center of the first section page and occupying a quarter of the page space, Doug saw a full color picture of a beautifully restored, jet black steam locomotive. The headline above the image said:

Body Found in Bensenville Engine

Firebox Becomes Crematory

Underneath, a twelve-point caption told the story: "Bensenville PD spokesperson Cindy Grady today confirmed that police are investigating the discovery of a charred body inside the boiler of a restored Milwaukee steam locomotive. Cooling its boiler for repairs since its arrival in Chicagoland last week, the locomotive appears to have been used as the preferred place to end the life of a male subject, about whom authorities have released no other information except that the man was well-dressed and appears to have been in the engine for an indeterminate time. Anyone who has information for police, or who saw smoke coming from the parked engine, is asked to contact Crimestoppers. Tribune reporters contacted the owners of the engine, a group of private investors out of Boston, who declined comment."

"I didn't see this headline until after I left the warehouse," Charlie stated. "But I saw this locomotive on that model train layout."

"Body and all?"

"No, not body and all, at least I never opened up the firebox to see if there was a little charred piece of plastic inside. It's just that it was prominently placed so that anyone who noticed the little diorama with the narrow gauge locomotive— me, for instance—wouldn't be able to avoid seeing the model of the Milwaukee engine. Without a doubt, this engine was built and placed on the layout to represent the second steam locomotive murder."

"Could be just coincidence." Doug didn't seem as surprised by this information as Charlie thought he should be, and he made a note to avoid telling Doug too much more without somehow checking him out. After all, it had been a long time between acts for the two of them. Who knows how desperate Doug had gotten during his recovery from the flesh-eating bacteria. Armed independent contractors—we used to call them mercenaries—were known to have contact with all kinds of customers. Checking out Doug's activities would be hard and take time without the help Charlie had come to rely on from Linda.

It bothered Charlie that Angelo Testa seemed to be admitting to the murders, and taunting Charlie with the information, while, the whole time, Charlie had no evidence against Testa. He knew that the two locomotives and the little figures would be gone if he went back. And if he confronted

Testa, it could be all over for sure, so he addressed Doug's lazy coincidence remark. "I'm just being paranoid."

"You're asking?"

"No, I'm telling you what you're thinking," Charlie faked, and then changed the subject. "So how about the Four and a Half Gang? Anything?"

Doug relayed the new information and sounded honest enough. The men were all identified though the DNA database; they were all ex-cons with rap sheets in big cities, with the common denominator being Chicago. No records in New Mexico or California, which, Charlie noted, made it likely they were only hired for the job of derailing the train to get at him. Their arrests read like a slippery slope of criminality, starting with burglarizing coin laundries and ending at armed robbery, assault, kidnapping, and attempted murder. They wouldn't have lasted long in Chicago without somebody from organized crime noticing or trying to recruit them. Two of the three had tenuous street gang connections, but didn't just about everyone who had been to Statesville?

"Gravel Gertie is a whole different story," Doug observed. "No match on any databases, and she ain't talkin'. Once the doctors pulled the slug out of her and got her off the morphine, she clammed up."

"I would have thought Busty Betsy. But Gravel Gertie is good. I get it. It's the throaty voice. Holding that gun, she looked and sounded like she was channeling Spawn of Satan." Charlie made small talk, not believing for one minute that whatever her name was didn't have a police record— somewhere. Either Doug was lying to him, or somebody was lying to Doug. "And she's a mean one."

Charlie's friend quickly caught his hesitation. "Look. That's what I was told," he angrily noted, even though he knew that a blank record for somebody found running a criminal operation was doubly suspicious.

"I've called in most of my favors with CPD, and DHS doesn't owe me shit, except for my fee," he continued. "Unless you can get your judge friend to open some doors, I'm afraid you may have to go begging to Terwig." The universal nickname used by officers for their top cop, Aloysius Terwilliger Garrity, had come to signify a Chicago officer who clung to power through a combination of political connections and never proven corruption. Terwig had been climbing the ladder when Charlie left CPD and had now been sixteen years in the position of Superintendent. Through those years, he had managed to piss off those who honestly rose to the ranks immediately beneath him to such a degree that the mayor had to step in. Chicago's mayor pushed through a city council resolution to eliminate the positions of Assistant Superintendent and Deputy Superintendent just to stifle those ambitions. Terwig had been no friend to Charlie, and, at least in Charlie's mind, figured heavily in his decision to leave CPD all those years ago.

"What's Terwig got to do with it?"

"Once the United States prosecutor found out that the whole operation was more an effort to get at you than it was terrorism, they turned Gravel Gertie over to CPD.

"You're kidding!" This didn't make sense to Charlie, because the best you could expect from a local prosecutor was some kind of wussy plea deal. "I expected incompetence from out west, and maybe even from a gutless fed paper-filer. But this case isn't going to get solved by charging people with stealing bubble-gum and then asking mother may I. What the f...?"

"I'm just the messenger." Whether real or feigned, Doug looked angry. "And don't think I'm not hearing you saying that I'm one of the gutless. I'm done for now." Charlie's long-time friend got up, threw down a greasy paper napkin, and said, "Lunch is on you!" Charlie got up, but Doug Christie's back was turned and walking out before Charlie could say anything. He fought the impulse to follow his friend and kick ass out on the street, but, if his admittedly skewed perception of this case was right, an assault charge putting him in lockup and his license in jeopardy could be just what the person pulling the strings wanted. So he let his hand go white knuckled holding onto the chair back while forcing his butt back into his seat.

Cooling off while he counted out enough money to cover a tip and the check, a check that had materialized on the table while he wasn't paying attention, he mulled over whether to approach Terwig. On the one hand, if CPD wanted to build a local case against Gravel Gertie, somebody could easily drag Charlie in as a material witness. On the other, if he waited for that to happen based only on what he already knew, the murder case—make that cases now—could go down the drain while he passed up a chance to interview his assailant. And that could also be exactly what somebody wanted to happen. Oh, well. Terwig had once criticized Patrolman Komensky for not being chummy enough with his commanders. Maybe he'd offer the guy dinner or something.

(CHICAGO POLICE HEADQUARTERS, FRIDAY, OCTOBER 12, 2:00 P.M. CDT)

It took Charlie twenty minutes to drive back downtown to police headquarters. The surprise was that it took less time for him to be admitted to the Office of The Superintendent. It seemed like Terwig was expecting his visit, and he said so before shaking hands with the portly head cop.

The public never saw anything but the uniformed Supt. Garrity of the 8 by 10 glossy Police Hall of Fame, or the occasional press conference or news photo op. By contrast, Terwig's daily garb was that of a police detective: Dark grey business suit and white shirt under an ample cut jacket to allow for a firearm, well-shined leather shoes, conservative pinstripe clip-on tie, and gold badge and wallet slung from the jacket pocket. Terwig's red, clean-shaven face seemed in part caused by the too-tight collar of his shirt, but, with red-veined nose, also clearly came from the owner's penchant for unwinding from a hard day's work with dark ale and Irish whiskey. Charlie wondered how many ambitious precinct captains secretly wished that just one more lamb chop would put Terwig in the bypass ward at Northwestern and double their chances of promotion at the same time.

Terwig didn't answer, but rather took the time to arrange himself comfortably in his desk chair and then look up at Charlie. "Don't just hover there, Komensky. You're the private dick here. If you're doing your job right, you should already know who's expecting you and who isn't." The top cop slouched to one side and leaned on an elbow as though trying to relieve gas, but he still kept looking at Charlie.

Finally, Charlie decided to take a seat on the plush sofa that nestled on a side wall between a bookcase and a set of trophy shelves. It suited him to keep his back to a wall instead of to the door. He got comfortable and stared back at Terwig.

"I got the message," he finally said. "You're holding the busty baritone broad, and I've got need for some answers." He stopped short of accusing the powerful cop of taking orders from criminals, but came close by saying, "And my detective skills tell me you have the incentive to let me get some."

Terwig reddened a bit, but wasn't fazed. "We hear you're looking into two murders."

"Word gets around."

"Your girlfriend in New Mexico did her job by checking you out with us."

Thanks, Bernie, he thought, and then asked, "Who squeaked about the second hit?"

"One too many of your former 'friends' entering their passcodes into one too many databases downtown. Need I go on? Or do you need names for some kind of vendetta?"

"No vendetta. I just don't like being manipulated."

"Well, here's manipulation for you." Terwig's face turned crimson and a vein started to pop on his forehead, like some underling was maybe going to get lucky in the promotion department. "I'll let you talk to the baritone bitch for a half hour. Then you've got forty-eight to tie her to your murders or she walks on whatever bail the bleeding hearts in Crimcourt decide to set. If you ask me why I'm doing this, your time with her goes down to fifteen minutes!" The Super noisily slid his top drawer out, grabbed a half full bottle of aspirin, and shook two directly into his mouth. Swallowing them dry, he choked slightly, then scribbled some instructions on a note pad, tore them off, and held them out to Charlie. "Don't make me get up to give this to you!"

(COOK COUNTY CRIMINAL COURTS BUILDING [CRIMCOURT], OCTOBER 12, 2:42PM CDT)

The tombs in the basement of the criminal courts building weren't any different than they had been when Charlie was a rookie. The only renovations that had taken place in fifteen years were those that gave the duty officers some typical post-911 protections, like metal detectors at the doors. The same concrete floors, same hard tile walls, same drab lighting, and the same stench of drug-soaked sweat, vomit, and urine that couldn't be washed out of the place with an ocean tanker of disinfectant laid hands on Charlie's senses and wouldn't let go. He'd had the experience before: It always took two or three days for food to start tasting good again. He'd have to burn his clothes.

Because of the sheer difficulty a suspect would have in escaping from the place—even if that suspect murdered his interrogators or took them hostage—security seemed lax compared to some of the smaller facilities he had been used to. Gertie sat in the ubiquitous metal chair behind a three by six table made from one-inch chipboard that sat on a pedestal made out of two three-inch steel pipes set into the concrete of the floor. The pipes came right up through the chipboard, which was held in place by pipe nipples below and caps above steel plate, so that even the strongest of felons would have required a large wrench to dislodge the board. The walls of the room were standard painted concrete block, with doors and two small one-way mirror glasses—no picture windows like in the movies—set deep into frames that were grouted just as deeply into the block. So much for fortress Cook County.

The broad herself, and Charlie thought of her that way, looked smug as she sat in her orange canvas jumpsuit, one leg shackled to a link set in the concrete floor, with her arms folded in front of her. The huge breasts heaved under the canvas. Somebody, a female guard, no doubt, had taken pity on her and given her a short strip of torn fabric to tie her blonde hair back. In this way, and in the harsh florescent lighting, he could see a terrible scar that extended from the hairline on her right temple down and back across the bottom quarter of her right ear, which was completely gone below the antitragus. She saw him staring and turned her head so he could see the continuation of the scar back along the side of her neck through the sternocleidomastoid area. "Ice breaker, huh?" she quipped, and Charlie realized that she had the slightest hint of a Western European accent that he hadn't noticed out in the railroad yards. It was also a bit of a surprise that she opened the conversation in such a casual manner.

"I had the impression you didn't want to talk."

"I got you to thank for not being deported." She swiveled forward and clasped both hands on the table, letting the full front of her face catch the light. The chain gave her a few feet to walk, but she didn't. Without the makeup she must have been wearing on the job, her face looked ugly to Charlie, in a challengingly sexual sort of way. "So we ain't got much time. Do you think they're recording us."

"In this stinkhole? So many dollars in sound equipment have gone bad down in this dampness that they can't beg for any more. They have to use a court reporter if they want to record anything."

"Hear that?" she suddenly yelled to nobody in particular. "Cop sez I ain't bein' recorded."

Charlie held up his hand in a stopping gesture. "I'm not a cop. Do you want to talk to a cop?"

"Don't be a shithead, Komensky, I want to talk to you. You don't think I'd be dumb enough to engage a target without knowing all there is to be known about it, do you? 'Cause if you do, then we're over here. Guard!"

"Wait, Miss . . . " He knew they'd have to tap dance.

"Ain't no miss and ain't no missus. If you need a name, call me Burgie." She pronounced the g softly, like it was a French name.

"Have you told the cops your name?"

"Ain't my name. It's got more to do with where I'm from. You figure it out, Eisenstein."

"You mean Einstein."

"Whatever. You want to discuss dead scientists or hear what I got to say."

Charlie leaned forward, which may have been half a mistake. Her breath smelled like egg that had been grilled with onions on a hot truck tire. "I'm all ears," he said. "No offense."

"None taken. But you gotta understand me." Her big right hand shot out and grabbed Charlie by the throat with tentacle-like fingers before he could parry. The fingers closed around his windpipe and said that the table wouldn't be so secure in her hands after all. "If I still wanted to finish the 'job,' your neck would be gushing blood right now." She released him with a shove that propelled him back onto the chair, which he prevented from going over backward by only the narrowest of margins.

Charlie coughed and choked up phlegm, feeling at the same time to see if his bruised neck really did have evidence that her fingernails had penetrated the skin. Finding none, he arranged his chair a little way back from the table where it would take her more time to strike. "Got it," he observed. "Somebody wanted me dead, and now they don't."

"Maybe they do, and maybe they don't. If you ask me, they just want to see you squirm."

This came as a surprise. It wouldn't have been the first time somebody sought revenge against him, and Charlie believed it would never be the last time until he was actually on the righteous slab in some crematory with his soul on the way to detective hell. A career in law enforcement doesn't get you thanks from most of the people you arrest. On the other hand, most of them didn't try to get revenge either. The vast unwashed majority were busy either getting their selves rearrested or getting their lives back together. The revenge minority probably consisted half of punks who were narcissists and thought that being the center of the known universe required no other universes to exist, or of the highly intelligent elite criminal who traded revenge cards for status and favors. If you could do revenge right, a lot of doors opened in the maze that was the lower echelon of the underworld. But he just didn't see the disconnected pieces of this case as something that looked like revenge on an aging Bohunk detective from Chicago.

"I never had anything to do with convicting diamond thieves," he reacted, probably saying just a little too much. "Why would you be telling me this?"

"'Cause I was supposed to get a free ticket, and now I hear from the grapevine that I won't even get paid!"

"That makes some sense, but not a lot. Who wants me to squirm?"

"Got anything to trade?"

"I don't have any deals to broker. Remember, I'm not a cop."

"I know who you are. You can get one."

He squinted and pretended to be thinking hard. "I have a friend who's a judge."

"Write it out and sign it." She slumped back into the chair and folded her arms again.

Charlie got up and knocked on one of the reverse mirrors. In a few seconds, he heard the clank of the outer door as it opened and closed, and then the inner door opened slightly with a black guard's face in the opening. Once Charlie had requested a pen and a few sheets of paper, and the guard had gone to get them, he turned to find Burgie seated on the table edge, legs crossed and leaning on her straight left arm in a relaxed pose that would keep the ugly scar on her ear and neck facing away from him. She had unzipped the front of the jumpsuit just enough to reveal the worn cotton prison tee that did yeoman work holding in the massive breasts that now undid her center of gravity. "What's with this broad?" he thought, but chalked it up to the best in prison seduction she could muster under the circumstances. She wanted to work him for a deal.

She leaned forward a little more as he walked back toward her, and as she did so her left hand slid close to one of the two pipe caps on the table top. "Want to play with the sisters while we wait?"

Noting how truly awkward this big, vile woman looked, and how unbalanced, Charlie just shook his head and looked away from the spectacle.

"Aw, common." She leaned even more, and her left hand touched the pipe cap. A pop like a .22 made Charlie turn, drop, and do a gun-reach. Bergie's left hand held onto the pipe like it was trying to crush it and let go of it at the same time, her eyes bulging in the sockets. Her mouth moved, soundless, and a slight smell of burnt hair touched his nostrils before she literally flew back from the table. An electric spark the length and thickness of a boa constrictor followed her, and a ripping sound split the stinking air. Bergie landed in a pile in the far corner, while Charlie heard the clank of the guard coming back. The look on the guard's face when he saw the smoldering heap of scorched orange jumpsuit said it all.

CHAPTER NINE

"Well what did you expect to happen?" Doug Christie had once again come through and posted bail for his friend, then followed him to the Bensenville railroad yards. "You were interrogating a suspect when she was almost killed by electrocution."

"Coulda been me," was all that Charlie said, focusing more clearly on the big, Northern-type steam locomotive that stood in the second track over from the platform where he and Doug were to be meeting with the president of the Friends of 1242. Despite unpredictable October weather, a perfect day for looking at a big steam engine had dawned pleasant and clear. Later that day, they could expect dry weather and a high near seventy, but, here at an hour past sunrise, the cool air and the high humidity allowed steam from the engine to condense in the air and form white billows that surrounded the engine and contrasted with the sleek, black paint on her sides. There could have been no more effective evocation of the glory days of steam railroading.

"I'll give you that, at least," agreed Doug. "But if you believe what Gergie said."

"Bergie; she said to call her Bergie."

"Okay, if she was telling the truth, she was going to spill who's behind all this. Wouldn't that be more likely?"

"I guess." Charlie sighed and wished he could just walk around and look at the big, hissing, thumping, whirring, knocking steam engine. He tried to get as much of the unique smell through his nostrils as possible, then he said, "But it's a hell of a way to commit a murder. How did the murderer know she would touch the hot pipe."

"Well, she ain't dead. But she sure is messed up. Maybe it was a crapshoot with the dice loaded. Any face that comes up is a winner. One way you shut up, the other way she does."

Charlie shook his head. "There's still too many variables. Either the person we're dealing with is awfully sloppy, or there's more than one Jack Horner with his thumb in this pie. Were you able to get anything from Terwig?"

"Are you kidding? If you or I cross his threshold this morning, he's going to see to it that the closest thing either one of us ever does to police work is clean the toilets in the sub-basement. But I did get one of my contacts in County Hospital to open up. Your ugly dame spoke two words to the attending before they sedated her to relieve the pain of partial electrocution. But I don't think they mean anything."

Charlie looked down the platform and saw the figure of a bald man with a grey fringe in blue coveralls coming toward them. "Our meeting's almost here. What'd she say?"

"Don't hang your hat on this," said Doug. "She said, 'Way hot.'"

The man with the grey fringe materialized out of the hot engine steam holding a striped Kromer engineer's cap in one hand and a leather bag, a little like a doctor's bag, in the other. The Kromer was authentic. At one time, in the heyday of steam, every engineer had owned one at least once. He had on comfortable looking shoes. The hint of an unshaved beard on his angular jaw was also grey, but his blue eyes twinkled almost like a Santa. They looked squarely at Charlie, and a smile of recognition broke across the man's weathered face. He donned the cap and held out a hand in greeting. "Charlie, you miserable expletive deleted, you're still getting me into all kinds of trouble."

Charlie introduced Judge Elmo Burmeister, retired, to Doug, who mumbled something about Charlie having a guardian angel. At about five foot ten and unable to keep his weight below two thirty, the judge didn't look as well-kept as most judges on or off the bench. Like Charlie, he liked to get his hands oily and didn't mind coal dust under his fingernails. The look of a common laborer belied his almost thirty years on the bench before retirement. "Charlie, you didn't tell me your guy also ran a railroad," commented Doug, seemingly uncomfortable with the situation.

"Just a special interest group," Burmeister corrected. "You didn't think Charlie would be able to solve this one without some information on the second victim of the Steam Locomotive Murders."

Doug gulped and looked a bit put off by the surprise. "Guess not. I was just filling him in on my connections."

The judge put down his engineer's bag and put his left hand on Doug's shoulder. "Don't be jealous. Connections in this business flow in and out like the tide in Cathlamet Bay." The reference was to a bay on the Columbia River near Portland where the judge had grown up, and Charlie felt the need to explain this to Doug, but the judge held up his hand. "My family history will have to wait. I've got to do a serious prep inspection on this baby, and we've got an all aboard at nine. Don't want to miss my chance at the throttle."

Charlie knew the judge had a steam engineer's license and hoped he'd be able to get one someday as well, but decided to stick to the investigation. "What did you get from Bensenville PD."

"Oh, they've just about washed their hands of the matter. Cook County Sheriff took over and released the locomotive last night. The coroner is dead certain that the body was in the boiler long enough to destroy any useful forensic evidence on the locomotive herself. The authorities along her route have been notified to look for evidence where the locomotive stopped; that's a longshot. Most of her stopping points were in high traffic areas with lots of fingerprints and footsteps, vehicles coming in and out, people taking pictures, and so on. We haven't sent out a call for witnesses, but that's an option. Nobody here in Cook County wants to incur the expense of answering all those crank calls for a murder that probably occurred in another state. Best guess, based on the schedule she's been keeping, was during a stop in San Berdoo on Tuesday."

"That's where they keep the Santa Fe engine, isn't it?" As soon as he asked the question, which was rhetorical in any case, Charlie realized he'd run off topic and into the weeds. "Sorry, Elmo. You know how I get."

The judge just grinned. "I thought you'd want to go running off to San Bernardino." He paused long enough to let the sarcasm ring true. "Just in case there was a chance to solve a case, of course. So here's the story. And you didn't get it from me." Judge Burmeister laid it out quick and fast, the way Charlie liked to get information. Doug would be uncomfortable without a notebook, but not Charlie, who was used to remembering information on the fly. Even, so, Doug looked squirrelier than he had yesterday.

The body had a name, and it was doctor: To be precise, Dr. Lynwood O'Brien, a private practitioner in cosmetic surgery in Thousand Oaks, California, for about five years, from '99 until mid-'04. The identity came from a card for a medical society found in a badly deteriorated and otherwise empty wallet and was confirmed by radiography on the right arm showing a compound fracture automobile crash injury O'Brien had suffered in his pre-teen years. As with the lawyer, the corpse had been shot before the murderer had tried to turn him into so much boiled meat. Except this time, there was a slug to run ballistics on. No answers yet, though. No boiler wash was found in the corpse.

O'Brien had set up his practice right out of medical school, and there had been a board enquiry about the source of his funding. Nothing ever proven. Then he unexpectedly shuttered the clinic and went off grid, to the great dismay of his sometimes inadequately face-lifted patients. Until now.

Charlie's mind raced. A doctor could have had access to the injection gun used on the first vic, but then who murdered the murderer?

"One more thing." Judge Burmeister put a firm right hand on Charlie's arm and held it tightly. "I don't suppose you'd know anything about this," he said, almost sarcastically. The high-def picture he showed Charlie on the smart phone in his other hand was of a stone almost identical in apparent size and shape to the one Charlie still had in his pants pocket. "It was in the victim's shoe."

(FLYING OVER THE SOUTHWEST, SUNDAY, OCTOBER 14, 7:21 A.M. CDT, BY CHARLIE'S WATCH)

Charlie didn't see how anyone could tolerate regular air travel. As recreation, he could see it: Soaring higher than the clouds with a bird's eye view of everything below, including railroad lines and trains, he got the same godlike feeling that he had when standing near a really good model train layout, like the one in the warehouse on Jasper Place. That's where it ended for Charlie, though; because ten minutes before any commercial flight he started feeling like the sweat-drenched victim of some sort of cruel reality show where the participants earn points for the number and degree of insults, embarrassments and discomforts they can stand up to in addition to paying to be on the show. Additional points could be earned for keeping one's bladder intact during a Chicago-L.A. flight into a 200 knot headwind with three commodes out of service and the plane's wings flapping like a Victoria's Secret costume on a model with one short leg. Fortunately, this flight was not as bad as that, and, with an aisle seat and only one other passenger on the row, he had time to doze and think on the just over two-hour, early Sunday flight to Albuquerque.

If he didn't go at least half way by air, he wouldn't be in San Bernardino until sometime on Wednesday. He had toyed with taking the Southwest Chief all the way out to L.A., and then he wasted Saturday night breaking into the former law offices of Dinwiddie and Maynot, somehow transformed into Wexler, Maynot and Fikru Law Group, LLC. Speaking of half way, about half way through that escapade, he wondered if Bergie was trying to pronounce Maynot instead of way hot. He wasn't proud of committing a B & E, and knew that he could never share it with Judge Burmeister, who took a dim view of solving crimes by committing others, but he also knew that a Saturday night was the best time to hit a lawyer's office. If discovered at all, the crime would not be reported until early Monday morning, after the senior partner had visited the health club and was available to discuss what was compromised and decide whether to report any crime at all. As long as you took only client information from lawyers, and not jewelry or cash, most wouldn't take the risk that a police investigation would uncover dirty laundry of the most embarrassing kind.

The first thing he had done after jimmying the front door lock was search for lawyer names in the firm's human resources files. None of the current or past associates of the firm appeared to have a Belgian name, though Charlie would be the first to admit to no competence in determining a nationality from a name beyond the Czech and Polish names he'd learned as a child. Fikru might have been anything except that the firm's letterhead said they had an affiliate office in East Africa. He'd found no file on Dinwiddie, but he didn't know if that was significant or not.

Charlie shifted in his seat and cursed the fact that this was the kind of research he'd been relying on Linda to do. Despite an open laptop and an active Internet connection on the flight, he wasn't sure whether Eritreans mined diamonds or used them for drilling for oil. So still no connection between Antwerp diamonds and the law firm, but it was worth some more digging. At this rate, without Doug or Linda doing some legwork, he'd have to find enough free cash to hire an assistant.

Dinwiddie's old firm's client list read like a who's who of Chicago crime, with a slight leaning toward South Side gangs and a few names Charlie recognized from Berwyn. Charlie's skin crawled at the thought of dealing with some of these names again. He'd arrested several of these guys, and prosecuting attorneys had even managed to convict a few back when Charlie was on a vendetta. He didn't like to think about those days. He had been a Chicago cop and his motivations had been more focused on jailing crooks than on living his life.

Angelo Testa appeared among the names, but infrequently and related to tax matters. Many of the client files went back to a time when Dinwiddie was with the firm, but as detailed a reading as Charlie could muster without spending the night suggested that Dinwiddie did nothing for his fees. Charlie knew that there were lawyers out there who just did research, but he doubted any would be name partners in a law firm. Thinking about it now, on the flight, he was sorry he hadn't pumped Medical Investigator Speeno's memory a bit harder. The only other answer was that Dinwiddie had been purged from the records, and probably purged recently.

Monday night in L.A., Charlie would have to go through the client lists he had managed to copy and—again without the direct resources that Linda and Doug provided—try to establish any connections that made sense. What did Antwerp diamonds, Dinwiddie, an amazon named Bergie, and a plastic surgeon from Thousand Oaks have in common with Angelo Testa? He wished that Georgio had tailed him onto the plane just so he could simply ask Georgio that simple question. Then an idea occurred to him: If Charlie could talk his way into a ride on the big Santa Fe engine, one with an invited guest, maybe he could buy some info from Testa with the promise of a half hour in the engineer's seat. He fell asleep with a dream of running a steam locomotive across Cajon Pass.

(ALBUQUERQUE, NEW MEXICO, SUNDAY, OCTOBER 14, 7:21AM MDT)

The airline got him to the Albuquerque International Sunport on time and over budget, giving him a while to grab a sandwich and snoop around the Barelas rail yards where the mid-twentieth century's premier passenger railroad, Santa Fe, had serviced the big steam engines that took premium trains like the Super Chief, and premium personalities of the day over Raton Pass into Colorado. Ever since the last week's short visit to the Albuquerque station, he'd wanted to get a better look around the old facility. The deterioration of the site worried him. His railfan's nose, able to see the old footings where others just saw concrete fences, told him that the entire roundhouse had been removed, though the turntable remained. Other significant artifacts, such as a transfer table that served 24 tracks in the erecting hall, back shops, and car shops, seemed to be in danger of dissolving into the desert dust that covered everything. What a prize for somebody like himself who, given the money, would gladly use such a facility to preserve and restore steam locomotives from anywhere they could still be found restorable. Depressing as it may have been, Charlie had to concede that its atmosphere was better than the transit center, which had a bus terminal in it. Sacrilege!

Charlie's depressed, train-tainted brain kept him from seeing that Georgio actually had followed him to Albuquerque. In fact, Georgio was having trouble understanding why this crazy detective would spend an hour wandering through what, to Georgio, seemed nothing more than a junky museum of urban blight as bad as any he'd ever seen in Chicago. He was relieved when Charlie finally sat down at the transportation center, where a weary wise guy could take a leak and get Snickers from the vending machines.

Bad luck, he couldn't sit down and enjoy it, because Charlie was on the move before he could peel open the wrapper. Relieving the bladder would have to wait.

Without missing a train, since the very first days when the railroad's promotions had started a boom in travel to the Southwest, the Indians had been selling Indian pawn, jewelry, and turquoise on the station platforms in Albuquerque. As a bona fide railroad geek, Charlie liked to see this phenomenon and visit with the sellers. He'd done a little of it last time, and needed to do more, just as much as he would have needed to see smoke billowing from a hot steam locomotive if one were on the way. He'd never been able to come up with enough dough to make a real buy, but today he considered it. The situation with Linda hadn't seemed as dire last week, but now, who knew? A trinket or two to take back as a peace offering for Linda could be a good idea.

He had the time before the train arrived, he reasoned to himself. He could stroll south along the folding tables and blankets laid out on the platform in a long row. Not all of the jewelry was Indian, of course. The trade had become tainted by the commercial jewelers. The average tourist didn't know turquoise from tortoise, and the possibility of making a quick buck on a cheap trinket off an unsuspecting traveler didn't put a nick in the backside of an Indian seller's conscience.

The sudden glint of sunlight off what looked like a diamond bracelet buried in the piles of silver and turquoise on one seller's Navajo blanket gave Charlie an idea: Had either of the victims ever done business here? Charlie had managed to get printouts of the victim photos to carry with him. To him, a suspect photos on a so-called smart phone made as much sense as a DVD player in a police cruiser. He'd seen both, but never particularly wanted to use either. Doing it the old-fashioned way, he started methodically walking from the near end of the row of vendors, showing the photos to each man or woman, never noticing Georgio following him from a safe distance, no longer thinking about Linda or that appeasing trinket.

Between getting each Indian seller's attention—Charlie knew he should think of them as Native Americans but couldn't help thinking "Indian"—and keeping that attention, it took him a half hour to get to near the end of the row. The train would be in soon, and all that the sellers would focus on then would be making a sale. The whole exercise seemed futile, but a detective needed to be methodical, and he would finish and walk back north, if need be, covering the row again as long as the Chief failed to pull in on time and interrupt. What was he thinking? Amtrak on time?

He was holding the print out at arm's length waiting for a crusty looking seller in a dark red shirt and dusty jeans to stop leaning over his table when the man looked up. Charlie realized almost immediately that he couldn't tell, short of his being crusty in the worst possible sense of the word, how old the man was. Crusty could have been sixteen or sixty, and, when he looked up, he stood at about Charlie's height. The seller had cold, grey eyes, no facial hair, and brown skin with a shiny-wrinkled look like the upholstery on a recliner lounge that had seen too many televised football games. His short-cropped hair, almost the same color as his face, grew abundantly on the sides of his head, but had become thin and slightly kinky on top. He suddenly grinned, grabbed a business card off the table, and held it out to Charlie. "Hi, I'm Dennis Hunt. I'm guessing you're either looking for a missing relative or you're some kind of cop. Here, take this." That the seller did not grunt his sentence like Tonto surprised Charlie.

Taking the card, he noticed that it said Dennis Hunt, Pueblo Jeweler, and had an address with an unpronounceable name—something like toe-jam-leaky-gee—and no phone number. He held out the victim print again and demanded, "You seen these guys?"

"Lemme see again. I used to be pretty good at this."

"Good at what?"

"Recognizing gringos that came through here a lot."

"So you know one of these guys?"

"Can't put a name to him," he said grabbing the paper and pointing to the doctor. "But I think he's the guy used to get off the northbound and buy a lot of things from Jimmy Lee."

"I take it Jimmy's a Jeweler, like you?"

The Indian tilted his head back and squinted at Charlie. "What you want this gringo for?"

"I don't. Mr. Gringo is mucho dead. I just want to find out who killed him."

Again, the Indian looked askance at Charlie. "The word you're looking for is *muerto*, and stop with the damn idiom, already. I'm from Chicago, like you. You think Jimmy did it?"

"Unless Jimmy's in San Bernardino, no, I don't—and good guess, by the way."

"Not a guess. Lot of people get off the trains here." Hunt handed the print to Charlie. "Haven't seen Jimmy in six months, but his family lives in San Filipe. Just take the freeway north and follow the signs."

"Have any steam trains been through here lately?"

"Now you a mucho loco gringo." Hunt smiled and went back to his table, leaning over his wares in the position Charlie had found him in.

Charlie chuckled to realize that the tourists would never know their Indian jeweler had probably learned the craft from somebody like Nate Steinmetz.

Now the decision for Charlie to make was whether to postpone the railroad leg of his trip to go track down an Indian who hadn't been seen in six months, or to continue the journey and double back later, if necessary. Logic told him that he'd waste a day just finding the pueblo, and that most of the people there, and the pueblo authorities, if any, wouldn't be as forthcoming with information as Dennis Hunt. A good detective relied on his sources, and the only source Charlie had in New Mexico was a Taos County deputy. Before returning to Chicago, he would have trusted her implicitly. Now he wasn't that positive.

The westbound was just nosing into the station when he got another idea. Charlie's last murder case had involved the death of an Indian named Sharedream, and the lead cop on the case was a police sergeant from Iowa City named Arnie Whittaker. Maybe Arnie could shake the Native American community bushes there and see if anyone has a friend up on the pueblo. The phone call was short and to the point, putting only a couple minutes on his phone. Arnie would do what he could. Once he hung up, he regretted sharing the information even more than he regretted that he didn't have the balls to call Linda instead. He preferred getting information from law enforcement, not giving it; but, without Linda, everything was a little off.

(Aboard The Southwest Chief, Monday, October 15, 2:07 a.m., MDT)

Any good railroad fan, and Charlie was one of those, deplored the state of the American passenger train. Government control and government subsidy had done its best—as it had in many other areas of American life—to rot the once vibrant system of the American passenger train from the core out, so that it survived not only at the mercy of politics but at the mercy of the freight railroads. The railroads, after all, just wanted to turn a profit for their stockholders, and had been doing so by investing billions with a big B on infrastructure and freight terminal capacity. As much as many people preferred riding the passenger trains, those people weren't shippers of freight, for the most part, so passenger trains were just the gnats that irritated the railroad's dispatcher until he or she could swat them flat into a siding and let the priority freights roll by. Charlie understood that, but at two in the morning, this delay was just a bit more irritating than usual. Unable to sleep, and full of heartburn from the greasy steak he'd gulped down alone at the diner's last sitting, he strode the platform at Gallup trying to will the signals ahead of the train to turn green. Gallup showed as a fuel stop on the schedule. The refueling service, consisting of a tank truck and two half-asleep men in hardhats, had fueled the two big P42 locomotives at the time of their arrival had long since departed. That had been 8:30, when they should have been almost to Winslow. A few diehard passengers had taken to the cold night until the reality of cold at high altitude had forced them to reconsider the warmth of even a non-moving Amtrak coach. Now, the big diesels sipped the new fuel and uninterestingly growled on while only a group of two trainmen and a local railroader in a hardhat with the logo for *BNSF Railway* huddled near the engineer's cab.

Our detective passed them as he strolled to the west end of the asphalt platform. It met the ground at a ragged point beyond which the ground disappeared into the night like a Star Wars credit roll. Only the silvered rail tops of the main line reflecting the signals from a mile away gave any hint that the ground continued beyond the platform, and he didn't feel like stumbling into a rattlesnake hole while finding out. From this vantage point looking north, Charlie could see some high mesas topped by random lights, he assumed from houses. Behind him, the Mother Road, Old Route 66 through Gallup, didn't carry much traffic, or have very bright lights at that time of day. Below the mesa, big truck rigs lit up like Christmas trees identified Interstate 40, the only road through Gallup that did have traffic. Above the mesa and the lights of the houses, he could see the North Star. Turning and looking up, he saw the Milky Way splashed across the sky from the other side of Mother Road to just overhead. Even the endlessly revved head-end generators of the Amtrak locomotives didn't completely drown out the Interstate noises that echoed across the town from mesa to mesa.

Charlie looked at his watch and, seeing only a hairy wrist, realized he had left it in the room. Pulling out his cell phone, he confirmed the time, then jumped as it rang with his old-time telephone ringtone. The three men near the engine looked up, and Charlie smiled sheepishly to account for the disruption of the otherwise imperfect silence. It was Whittaker, and he took the call. After explaining that he'd only made it as far as Gallup from Albuquerque, he accepted the intel offered by his old pal. Jimmy Lee had a cousin named Wayna Walter who worked as a kind of guide on board the train to describe scenic features and add a little color like the old Santa Fe guides from the 1930s. One of the tribal registries had them both in California in the past six months.

No new licenses or registrations for either Jimmy or Wayna there, but it seemed normal to Whittaker for Native Americans to avoid complying with anything but tribal laws. In the back of his mind, Charlie wondered how a guy like Whittaker would do in Gallup, where Indians outnumbered everyone else.

Eager to talk to the trainmen before the train got going again, Charlie abruptly said, "See if any of the usual gem or precious metal outfits have a certificate on either one with a current address. And Arnie? Thanks for the middle of the night update." He didn't wait to see if Whittaker had any small talk to make and ended the call.

The two trainmen tried to ignore Charlie's close approach until he was right on top of them, then the taller of the two, wearing an Amtrak blue coat and a conductor's hat, turned and said, "Think we'll be another half hour." Tall and thin with a long face with a nose credibly long enough to give the face balance, cheeks made rosy by the cold, a well-trimmed mustache and eyes that said he needed three days' sleep, the conductor tried to turn back, but Charlie stopped him.

"Do you know Wayna Walter?"

"You mean Wayna get drunk and never come back to work Wayna?" snapped the conductor. "Or Wayna play poker really bad on layover and still owe Conductor Bob five hundred bucks Wayna."

Charlie shrugged. "Yeah, probably that last guy."

"Sorry, and you are?"

"Looking for him and his cousin Jimmy."

"Never mind, I know who you are from the passenger manifest. I'm just surprised that a guy from Chicago knows Wayna. Far as I know he never traveled east of Lamy."

Most times, Charlie never felt the need to let his business be known unless it freed up information, and this was one of those times. He detected a slight odor of rye on Conductor Bob, whose name badge said his last name was Steuben, and deduced the trainman was loose-lipped enough to continue the conversation over more. He'd picked up the half-pint in a place called Nickels—half dive bar and half sandwich shop—on his way from the airport to the train station, and he pulled it out and offered it to the Conductor now. The other two railroaders pretended they didn't see it while Conductor Bob took a slug and handed back the hooch. "So where you think he is?" nudged Charlie in a secretive voice.

"Got off the train in Los Angeles and that's it. None of the crews have seen or heard from him since. Friend in human resources says he didn't have direct deposit and never picked up his last two checks. Funny. He was always looking for ways to make a buck. Son ' a bitch!"

Charlie had slowly walked back east along the train consist, cleverly separating Conductor Bob from the other two men so he could offer another drink. The trainman took it eagerly. "Don't think we'll be out of here before sunrise," he said revealingly. "Wreck ahead."

"What happened to a half hour?"

"It's what we say to all the passengers. You, sir, deserve the truth in return for the rest of that bottle. I need the sleep, and you, all things apparent, seem to have a need to find my deadbeat friend."

Following Charlie back into the vestibule of the Superliner car, the conductor explained that his network of railroad connections had put both Wayna and Jimmy Lee in Barstow the week before last. Charlie gave him the rest of the bottle, and then turned to go back to his room.

Charlie stopped suddenly and turned back. "One more thing and I'll let you hunker down. Has DHS ever rousted Wayna about anything?"

"Funny you mention it, but on his last trip they did."

"Who else knew about it?"

"Just me. I had to call Walter into the crew dorm for questioning. The DHS guy didn't want me to alarm any passengers, I guess. All right with me, though."

"Guy?" asked Charlie. He knew DHS traveled in pairs. "Where'd he board?"

"'S funny. I never noticed. An' the agent wanted me out of the car, so I never asked. Think that scared Wayna off?"

Charlie answered with another question. "What did the agent look like?" Then he listened as Conductor Bob gave a detailed description. The description vaguely fit both Nicholas Ramunda and Georgio. "I don't suppose you've seen the DHS guy since." Conductor Bob shook his head. Now Charlie took out his victim printout. "Were either of these guys ever on your train with Walter or the DHS guy?" Again the conductor denied he knew anything more.

Without remembering how they parted, Charlie found himself back in his compartment, thinking hard and fast and unable to sleep. Georgio wasn't just a messenger, but an integral part of the whole plot, whatever it was, to manipulate Charlie. Whether Georgio was also a murderer still remained to be seen, but he certainly was way ahead of Charlie as to how two Indians and dead Doc Botox knew each other. Trying to put all the pieces together, he turned again to the theory that he, Charlie Komensky, was supposed to be right there in the mountains of northern New Mexico when the lawyer's body was found, and that somebody either counted on Charlie to pocket the loose diamond or changed their plans to use his involvement when he did. Nothing beyond that made any sense, except . . . Did Georgio need him to solve the murder? And why? Logically, somebody connected with the Antwerp stones had to be pulling the strings. A double cross, maybe? Somebody needed to be murdered for revenge, or to silence them after all these years. Could he be involved just because he knew a Chicago jeweler who could identify the stones? Not impossible . . .

He fell asleep, and, after a time, a gross forward lurch of the train awakened him. He'd been dreaming a dream he'd never had before. In the dream, he walked through his mother's house in Chicago, and he knew he was a child. He looked through a doorway into their kitchen. Georgio, adult Georgio, stood in the kitchen telling his mother and another man whose face he couldn't make out something he couldn't hear. When Georgio saw Charlie, he slammed the door in Charlie's face. Awakened by the lurch, jammed into the berth, his face against the cold panel under the compartment window, Charlie knew the dream had to be significant. He just couldn't understand how.

CHAPTER TEN

Plan A had failed. It had been for Charlie to be in some cheap hotel in some Los Angeles suburb, wearing nothing but his shorts and a T-shirt, with a six pack of PBR and working through the Maynot client list. So where he was now, planwise, didn't even make it to the top half of the alphabet. On the other hand, he'd found Wayna Walter, whose pale, drained face topped the covers in the hospital bed in the airy room in intensive care, just two miles from the railroad yards in San Berdoo. He didn't think a Native American could get that pale. They'd taken the breathing tube out about ten minutes ago, and it looked like the surgery had successfully repaired the knife wound to the Indian guide's side. Non-critical or not, Walter had not regained consciousness since they had found him. A uniform from the San Bernardino PD stood outside the door, but only for protection of a material witness, and, as Charlie had learned, Walter had no outstanding warrants in California.

It had been something like nine hours since the strange Georgio dream had compelled him to short his ticket to LAUPT and get off the train at the San Bernardino station. Just a hunch, but it set off the series of events that had gotten him here, waiting for Walter to come out of it. He thought back on those hours on the train to see if he had missed anything. Besides having breakfast and lunch in the diner, both at first sitting, he managed to engage Conductor Bob in a few more conversations about his railroad connections and decided that Bob Steuben could be a useful source as long as he didn't lose his job for drinking on it. Sitting in his compartment watching the scenery in Cajon Pass, he formulated a plan to lure Angelo Testa to Los Angeles by using his connections with Judge Burmeister, and with the Northern New Mexico Railroad, to get somebody in San Berdoo to offer Testa a cab ride on the steam locomotive there.

His train made the usual stop at San Bernardino. Strongly certain, then, that Testa and Georgio were connected, he saw the cold steam locomotive parked on a siding next to the station. It was too much to resist; hence, the early exit from his comfy compartment. This steam engine was a little bigger than the Milwaukee locomotive, and certainly a lot bigger than the diminutive steam of the Northern New Mexico. A set of portable steps had been assembled and placed next to the cab of the former Santa Fe Northern type steam locomotive, and Charlie left his bag on the platform and climbed them up to the cab floor level to find two members of the local volunteer group putting new red paint on valve handles and shining the brass sides of pressure gauges. "Do you guys mind if I take a look around?" Both volunteers wore white hard hats, safety goggles, and orange visibility vests and looked to Charlie like they knew their safety training; but Charlie had talked his way into locomotives without any safety clearance before. "I can go get my clearance from my bag if you want."

The shorter of the two volunteers turned from his brass polish. "We'd prefer you just stay there on the step scaffold.

Lots of wet paint. Don't want you to send a cleaning bill to the society."

"I get it," agreed Charlie. "When you going to fire her up?" When the taller volunteer looked at Charlie as though he had just fallen off a freight train, Charlie added, "I just got off Amtrak 3 and haven't checked your Web page lately."

The tall volunteer had a long, skinny nose that just barely held up his goggles even with the elastic strap pulled so tight that they gave his face a very fish-like appearance. "Come back in the morning and we'll be topping her off and lighting the burners."

"I might not be able to." His mind wanted to put the guy's face together with the orange, black and white visibility vest and call the tall volunteer Nemo, but he held onto that and instead said, "Work and all. What did you say your name was?"

"Hal."

Now Charlie was thinking halibut. "Who would I have to speak to to arrange a cab ride, Hal?"

Before Hal could answer, a muffled but echoing moan seemed to emanate from the bowels of the engine. Charlie looked at both men, but they didn't seem very concerned. "That normal?"

"Sometimes with the temperature changes," Hal answered, but he didn't sound terribly confident in his assessment. "Old stay bolts. They creak and groan."

The short volunteer had a Hispanic look to him, and reminded Charlie of Mike Ortega from the NNMRR. "I suppose you get secondary smoke, too?" asked Charlie as he surveyed the inside of the cab. For a moment, the idea of talking somebody into a cab ride took second place to Charlie's fantasy of sitting in the engineer's seat and running this locomotive full throttle up the pass. He checked the controls and dials off in his mind. Throttle and reverse lever off in the right corner of the cab on the engineer's side, brake stand with engine and train brake to the left of the engineer, sand valve and injector valves within easy reach. The array of gauges on the backhead read out boiler pressure, water level in two redundant glasses positioned near the apex of the backhead, brake air reservoir, cylinder and reserve pressure gauges. Then there were the valves and levers for controlling blowers to increase draft and dampers to reduce it. If this had been a coal burning engine, there would have been a stoker and a foot pedal to open the butterfly-type fire doors. As an oil burner, the engine had smaller fire doors that could be opened with a lever operating a pneumatic assist; no need to shovel in coal, just to check the burners occasionally. Where the valves that operated the stoker might have been were others controlling the right amounts of air, steam and oil into the burners. There had to be steam to atomize the oil into small, burnable droplets, so an oil burner starting cold would have to have an available, stationary source of air or steam to run the atomizer. Other valves let steam into coiled pipes in the tender to pre-heat the heavy "Bunker C" oil.

Charlie realized there was more to it than that. For instance, the fireman might have to shovel sand into the fire to clean soot from flues to increase heat transfer; and despite his fixation on the old days of steam, Charlie knew that this engine was probably being run on vegetable oil or recycled motor oil instead of "Bunker C." Stations and engine servicing facilities no longer had boiler steam readily available. He caught himself almost drooling before being snapped out of his reverie by the sound that caught all three men by surprise. "Heeeeeeeelp!" The weak groan echoed and reverberated through the heavy steel like a voice from deep inside a tomb.

He wasted no time taking the opportunity to jump inside the cab and hit the fire door lever. The two "wings" parted like a blooming flower, and Charlie peered in. "Get me a light!"

Before Hal or the other man could react, Charlie's eyes adjusted and he could see that there was some outside light coming up into the firebox from under the burners and grate. He could make out the form of a man lying on his side. "Heeeeeeeelp!" echoed again.

"Hold on and we'll getcha," replied Charlie as he realized he was too big to fit into the hole. The small volunteer was too hefty, as well, so Hal had to shinny himself in up to his waist. He managed to grab the man in the firebox by the ankle and start to drag him back as Charlie and Shorty pulled from behind; a piss poor way to conduct a rescue of somebody who was probably otherwise badly hurt, but there was no quick way in.

That put an end to any efforts on Charlie's part to get a free cab ride for his prime suspect, Angelo Testa.

At four hours plus twenty minutes there in the hospital, he realized that Walter was coming out of the anesthesia and called the officer at the door who then called his dispatcher and then came back into the room. The officer was a young, Hispanic man who looked capable, wore San Bernardino's state of the art uniform with the usual Sam Browne belt, what appeared to be a Glock in the holster, and heavy tactical-style boots. He had the stylish no-hair look that Charlie wished he could pull off, and seemed to be as fit and well-honed as a good straight razor. He spoke without any sign of ghetto lingo. "Detectives will be here shortly to find out who did this to you."

Walter fidgeted and looked even more distressed than he had been coming from the drugged state. Unable to form words, he raised his left arm with the IV, and, surprisingly, pointed at Charlie. The officer didn't catch on, but Walter finally managed to spit, "This guy!" Charlie's heart sunk immediately. It was a tight frame, and he was in the middle of it.

(SAN BERNARDINO POLICE DEPARTMENT, MONDAY, OCTOBER 15, 11:14 P.M. PDT)

It wouldn't have done him any good to run. The best result for the criminal who set this up, Charlie knew, would be for Charlie to go crazy and run and get shot and killed by one of his own. This being the third time on one case that he found himself on the wrong end of an interrogation room, at least he now knew it wasn't a bad coincidence.

But what an interrogation room! The single chair bolted to the floor could have been used for a waterboarding or an execution. No table for him to rest against, and instead of handcuffed behind him, his wrists and arms were pulled straight down at his sides and chained under the seat. The lighting, designed to be disorienting, came from just far enough behind him on both sides that he couldn't turn his head far enough either way to see its origin. The room was tall, too, maybe almost three times taller than it was square. No amount of light illuminated the high darkness above his head, from which the bare, unpainted concrete walls emerged, but not to complete clarity, before they reached the floor. If a ceiling hung up there, he couldn't see it. All he could do was shuffle his feet enough to know, for sure, that the floor was painted concrete. The single steel door with no panic bar also had no windows and merged with its jamb tightly enough to preclude putting a tool anywhere to pry it open, and circuit wires above the jam said, "alarm will sound," without benefit of a sign.

He'd been in situations before. Sometimes they were good to get his head out of the game long enough, while alone with his own thoughts, to discover something. Other times, they were annoying frustrations that kept him from doing the legwork necessary to solve the crime. This was a situation with a capital S. His protestations at the hospital had been feeble, of the "Why would I hurt this guy and then stand around waiting for him to finger me?" variety. As his Miranda warning was being read, he didn't listen; instead quickly telling the arresting officers details on where he'd been for the last 24 hours. And so far, it hadn't been enough to get him unshackled and back into the game.

They had his bag and his .38. That was no big deal; but this time Doug wasn't around to run interference, and the contents of his pocket, including the Antwerp (according to Nate) diamond, were also now in police possession. They would check his alibi and let him go, if not for that diamond, which would be a big, neon sign that said ARREST KOMENSKY. So while he cooled his heels and the rest of him—it was damn cold in the room—he just might as well use the time to take his head out of the game and think.

As good as this frame was, he had an alibi. Wayna Walter had to be pretty scared of whoever was doing the murders. Perhaps they had promised, if he fingered the good detective from Chicago, they would only rough him up a bit, and then "MacHeath" him so it wouldn't hit any arteries. But how did Walter know him? That leak in the Taos County Sheriff's Office? Speeno? Charlie takes the diamond and foils the murderer's plans to send a message, the murderer presumably being hooked in somehow with the Antwerp diamonds. So the murder fixates on Charlie? Too easy! It couldn't be that the diamond was never meant to be found, there was another diamond on the first vic, or at least Judge Burmeister said there had been. Otherwise maybe the lawyer was a courier and had had more diamonds on him, the diamond left with the body was accidental. But that would mean that either Burmeister was wrong or had been given the wrong information. By whom? A corrupt cohort of the corrupt Taos County deputy? Charlie ground his teeth and tugged at his chains. Whoever controlled Wayna Walter knew Charlie!

A flicker of the lights—just a moment of total darkness—interrupted his thoughts and made him reflexively tense up. Nothing of concern followed except for a beeping alarm that had been triggered somewhere in a distant part of the building he was in. He took a deep breath to relax and go back to thinking, but this time a loud metallic bang and the voices of two men arguing briefly stole his attention. The awkward position in the chair, though somewhat yoga-like, wasn't helping his concentration.

Awkward position! That may be it! Maybe somebody didn't put Walter up to fingering Charlie. Maybe he stabbed himself after crawling into the firebox! Good one! Charlie wanted to kick himself for being so focused on Testa that Wayna Walter completely fell off the bottom edge of his suspect list. "Guard!" he yelled. Why hadn't he checked for blood stains in the engine cab? Oh, yeah. The red paint. He also remembered the light coming up into the firebox from beneath the burners, grate and dampers. Damn crafty Indian could have crawled into the firebox, which would leave no blood in the cab, then stabbed himself in a predetermined place, and dropped the knife down into the grate. He'd have to ask the detectives if they had checked for a knife under the locomotive. "Guard!"

Twenty more agonizing minutes passed. Frustrated, tired, and just plain pissed, Charlie tried to think without benefit of notes and his laptop whether he would be able to put Walter in northern New Mexico or southern Colorado. What was it now? A week and a half ago? But then again, what did a gambling Indian guide know about hiring a three-passport, international goon like Nick Ramunda? If Walter was involved, he had to have a boss, who was also the goon's boss.

The heavy door opened, and the officer who had been at the hospital peered in and then gestured it safe for detective what's 'is face to come in. Charlie almost never liked his encounters with cops who thought they were his superior, and he guessed that this one would be no exception. First of all, the guy was wearing a full suit and tie, and he had a son-of-a-bitchin' mauve pocket handkerchief! "Butcher hook." thought Charlie. Second, Charlie had ten or fifteen years on the guy, who stood about six three and looked excessively fit, with traps that made his blue pinstripe suit stand down off his neck like a mink stole. Nonetheless, the well-tailored suit fit him as well as the clothes on any body builder, and the image was completed by his clean shaven face and short, neatly parted and combed blonde hair. Schwarzenegger of goddamn LGBT Berdoo PD! The detective stood menacingly in front of Charlie with a manila folder tucked into one hand and the other within striking distance.

"Mister Komensky." The first thing out of the cop's mouth said Charlie was wrong about which way his nightstick pointed. The deep voice came from places inside him that belied his appearance. Charlie knew those places: Dark, filthy gutters of human and human-caused misery that cops like this—and like Charlie hoped he had been—labor long hours with little thanks and less pay to drag into the cleansing light of day. The detective's voice was not without a little intentional roughness, a feigned harshness put there to buttress against any assault a suspect might initiate, but the burden of the misery and the sheer exhaustion of coping with it showed through in every word. Charlie only had but to look for them, and the signs of traumatic stress were there on the

face of this otherwise perfect specimen. "It appears you are—
or were—one of us."

"Retired detective from Berwyn PD." Charlie still had
every reason to expect that his alibi would stick.

"I'm Detective Lieutenant Jonas Petersen and you've
met Eddie Boggs over there at the door. He has instructions
to Taser you if you get out of hand. Looks like you're a better
detective than you are a criminal." Petersen waited for the
reaction that Charlie knew he had to refuse to have. Then he
said, "Southern States Air confirms you were on a flight from
Chicago to Los Angeles that got into LA yesterday afternoon."

"Not true, I flew to Albuquerque and took the train.
Check Amtrak."

Petersen looked again to see if there was any hint of
hesitation in Charlie's response. Finding none, he observed,
"Did that. Amtrak says nobody boarded yesterday in
Albuquerque."

"Nobody? You know that's gotta be wrong!"

"I just know what they told us." Petersen shrugged.
"Now you said you spoke to the conductor several times last
night?"

"That's right. Bob Steuben."

"According to Amtrak, the conductor on today's train
was named George."

Charlie almost pulled off his shoulders trying to stand
up; and uneasily flopped back into the floor-bolted chair. Cop
Boggs checked his impulse to restrain Charlie and remained at
the door. "You've got to check again." Charlie shook his
head. "I'm just out here to investigate. Were you able to get
in touch with Judge Burmeister?"

"Hasn't returned our calls."

"Keep trying."

"Komensky, I know you know how this game is played, but please don't issue orders. I'm not in the mood."

"Sorry. But you've got to realize that it's not possible that nobody got on in Albuquerque. It's just not normal!"

The detective walked around so that Charlie would have to turn his head sideways to see the detective out of the corner of his eye. Also part of the game, Charlie didn't bother. When his position failed to get an irritated rise out of his suspect, the detective walked back into Charlie's line of sight and said, "If it weren't for the troubling presence of a big, effing expensive diamond in your pants, I'd be inclined to believe that this was an expert frame up. Maybe even inclined to believe there's a good reason you have the diamond with you." He bent over until he was almost nose to nose with Charlie. "Is there a good reason?"

Charlie's next words were not what the detective expected. "Who else knows I have that?"

Petersen stood up full height. "Eddie here and about half a dozen San Berdoo cops working the case. Why?"

"Nobody outside the department?"

"Why?!"

"Do you trust your men?"

"Damn it, Komensky! Why?!!" Petersen became so red-faced it seemed to work its way up into the roots of his hair. "You saying I have something to clean up?"

Charlie looked at Boggs, who scowled back angrily, and then at Petersen's upset features. "I'm saying somebody had enough time to work out the frame since you valley boys put me in irons."

The detective stood up, gestured to Boggs, and both left the room. Charlie, alone to think about what had just happened, now knew that it wasn't his own paranoia he was dealing with. It was somebody trying to take him over the edge.

A half hour went by, during which Charlie heard no sounds from outside the interrogation room. It was as if the rest of the cop shop had been told to pipe down. Or maybe Detective Lieutenant Petersen had let it be known that he believed Charlie. Then he heard Petersen yelling at the top of his lungs out in a hallway somewhere, "Well damn it! It's got to be somewhere!"

Charlie had almost expected it. His gut told him that, since he'd been arrested, nobody was paying attention to Wayna Walter; and, furthermore, nobody took Charlie's story seriously enough that they would place extra security on a relatively valuable stone. With that piece of ice in police hands, it would only be a matter of time before he'd have to answer to possession of stolen property. Hell, he'd gladly answer questions about the diamond, but he'd just as soon the questions weren't coming from some FBI career climber with shit for brains. On the other hand, if it was now missing, as Petersen's outburst suggested, then there was the remaining question: Could they hold him?

The answer burst into the interrogation room with Petersen—sans guard. "Heard from your judge," he tersely mumbled as he unlocked the chains and dropped them on the floor behind Charlie. "Your paperwork is at the front desk. Leave a number where you can be reached."

Charlie stood up and stretched. It was good to be out of that position, though his bad leg still throbbed. "Where's the . . ."

"Let's just assume you'll find out, and leave it at that." The two men looked in each other's eyes and shared an understanding. No bad light would fall on the San Bernardino Police Department.

(Thousand Oaks, California, Tuesday, October 16, 1:56am PDT)

Charlie had slept badly in worse seedy lodgings than the motel in Thousand Oaks, where he flopped by necessity more than by choice after leaving San Bernardino that night. From what he'd seen of it on the way over, Thousand Oaks was upscale enough to not have any hotels like some he'd experienced, but the Value & Service Inn registered at least a six on the sleaze scale. He decided that he should be thankful that he'd gotten a room after eleven and that it had Wi-Fi that didn't crash when somebody in a neighboring room started streaming porn. Jammed in close proximity to Ventura Highway, an all-night In And Out, and a Witness Center where it seemed that the only thing to witness after midnight would be drug deals, the motel also registered above a five on the noise scale. No value and limited service was more like it.

But he had work to do, and had been sitting on his ass since getting there with the old leg wound aching, and no amount of Tylenol that would make it stop. After an hour on the www, he was into the third tier of Google pages on Antwerp, diamonds, and diamond heists.

As this case was trending, there was at the very least a compliant crook in the SBPD who looked the other way while a diamond gravitated back to its illegal owners. With the stone missing, that would make two PDs where somebody, or more than one somebody, couldn't be trusted. It suggested somebody behind this with money or power or both. Maybe that was a big red arrow pointing at Angelo Testa, but he had had no online luck in connecting Testa to anything but the usual gambit of American organized crime.

And what about those illegal owners? Charlie had to ask himself who they were. Was it somebody in the original gang that pulled the Antwerp job? From his Internet search, he now knew there had been several more recent attempts, some successful and some not, to score against the Antwerp. Some even as big as the big one that Nate had described. The most recent of these had been the past February, netting a cool billion in loose stones. None of the newest investigations pointed anywhere close to the old suspects, but some new criminals boldly pointed to the old Antwerp job as their inspiration! Almost made the theory that the motive for the Steam Locomotive Murders was a puny eighty million bucks seem like a shot in the wrong direction.

Was it somebody in the distribution chain? There would have been only three reasons for the haul to wind up in America. First, the idea man behind the whole job could be based in America. But that made the least sense, because money was money anywhere in the world these days. Second, there was perhaps a ready buyer in America that needed to have the physical diamonds, for some reason. With the stones marked as Nate said they were, that would mean cutting of the larger stones and selling off the smaller ones at a steep, steep discount. "Maybe," said Charlie to himself. "Too much speculation." Narcissistic criminals have done stupid things for worse reasons.

Finally, there was always a drug angle. Men high up in the drug trade often made unreasonable demands upon those who owed them money or, worse, favors. Maybe this was one of those unreasonable demands. Bring me $80 million in Antwerp stones, properly marked, and I won't cut out your right eye and feed it to your gerbil. It would be just like some lunatic drug kingpin who has all the money in the world to want to just spread the Antwerp diamonds out on the living room carpet before having S & M sex.

At almost 2 a.m., with two bags from In And Out laying on the desk chair, his laptop plugged in because its battery had long since died, and working furiously to try to tap into CJIS and LEO to get more information on drug dealers and diamond fences, Charlie heard a knock at the door. Before Charlie could copy and save some information, the knock got louder and more persistent.

With a deafening thump, the door abruptly slammed open against the side wall, knocking out drywall patch in the shape of a cheap doorknob. Georgio followed the door like a tank that had just flattened a thatch-roofed shack in some old Viet Nam War movie. The mobster had a small Smith & Wesson in his right hand and looked as though he'd gotten less sleep than Charlie. He immediately spotted Charlie's holstered .38 Special slung on the same chair with the burger garbage, and moved to stand between Charlie, who now sat on the bed with his hands up, and Charlie's gun.

The standoff between Charlie and Georgio promised to go on most of the rest of the night. Charlie didn't mind; he was used to going without sleep and would catch up later. The way he saw it, Georgio had no leverage, even though he had his pea shooter leveled at Charlie's chest. He could see that Georgio had done this before, as his right hand never wavered, and no additional fatigue showed on his face. He looked like he'd come prepared for Los Angeles weather, and was wearing a black T-shirt under a dark grey tweed sports jacket with frayed elbows. His summer-weight slacks were a slightly lighter grey, and he had on oxfords with woven inserts rather than the loafers he had been wearing during their last encounter.

Georgio closed the door and took up a tactical position at the foot of the motel bed. Also tactically, Charlie asked to be allowed to get dressed "I don't know where you're going to take me, but unless you let me put some pants on, I'm only fit for Walmart." He'd gotten on his Dockers and a Polo shirt before Georgio stated without emotion that they were staying right there in the room until Charlie told him what he knew about the $8 million in diamonds.

Charlie weighed the request and decided that it was the biggest revelation he'd gotten on this case since the beginning. It was confirmation of motive, but it was also confirmation that Georgio and his employer—perhaps Testa, perhaps not—were not the only interested parties. If they didn't know where the diamonds were located, which implied also the source of the diamonds found on the lawyer and the doctor, then Charlie deduced that there were other people who did. And now it was clear that they needed Charlie to stay in the game.

"Sooner or later, the arm's going to get tired." Not the best opener for Charlie, but a start.

"You'll be dead before then."

Not likely. At least they wouldn't shoot him here; and Georgio must have had no instructions to take Charlie anywhere else. Sitting at the head of his bed in a motel room, with both hands free, was decidedly different than wrapped in duct tape in a fetal position in the trunk of a sedan. Probably the reason Georgio had a pea shooter instead of a heavier weapon was he'd done this before. His mere presence was supposed to scare people into giving up info. "If I answer your question with an honest answer, you won't be happy with me," said Charlie finally.

"Try me."

"You asked me what I know of the location of $8 million in diamonds."

"Yeah?"

"It's complicated."

Georgio cracked a smile and shook his head. "Now you're just fuckin' with me."

"No. I'm dead serious. I think I now know where the diamonds WERE, but I don't know where they ARE. Will that make any sense to your boss?"

"Maybe. Paint me a picture."

"You first. Who are you working for?"

"You know already."

"Refresh my memory. What's your last name?"

"You really don't remember?"

"I remember a small card with an invitation to a gigantic, museum quality train show, with subtle hints that you and your boss were killing people. It made me think that you were the ones who had the diamonds, and you were eliminating competition and at the same time letting some of your rivals know who they were dealing with. But if I'm wrong . . ." Charlie was just fishing for information no matter what Georgio was up to. "Why should I remember your last name when I only met you a few days ago and you never told me your last name? Besides, my memory is better when I'm not at gunpoint."

Surprisingly, Georgio pocketed the gun and put both hands out in front of him. "I'm takin' a chance, here. But I need you to trust me."

"You gonna let me have my gun, too?" Maybe he was pushing it too far, but it was worth a try.

Again surprising him, Georgio stepped to one side and gestured for Charlie to get his .38 from the chair, and Charlie got up to comply. The gangster moved quickly, stepping to Charlie's side in one long stride. Charlie felt the sting of the needle at the base of his neck and the warm sensation as the drug entered his body. Before he blacked out, he remembered saying, "Shit! I hope it's not boiler wash."

CHAPTER ELEVEN

(INTERSTATE 40, NEW MEXICO, WEDNESDAY, OCTOBER 17, 12:50 P.M. MDT)

The dream made no sense, but on the other hand, when did a dream ever make any sense?

In the dream, Charlie sat in the living room of the old Chicago bungalow at 62nd and Menard. Although he had never been there since graduating from JFK High and moving into an apartment, he recognized the living room as the same furniture that his mother had managed to maintain after his dad died in '76. He looked around the room without looking around, as one does in dreams, and knew that he was an adult. He had access to all of the memories from the day of that graduation, from his police training, even the hotel room and Georgio, and the Georgio dream on the train.

Except, in the dream, it wasn't the present. The old RCA color set in the corner of the room played a baseball game, Goose Gossage pitching for the White Sox, and the game droned on while Charlie's father sat at the dining room table, visible from the living room through a wide arched doorway. The man seated at the table with his father was speaking to his father with Georgio's voice. Again odd, as he could also hear Georgio's voice coming from the TV—or from somewhere. Beyond that, everything familiar to Charlie—the gray sofa, the lounger in which he sat, the lamps, the laminate dining room set, the light gray walls—gave him a feeling of being at ease. He couldn't really hear what his father and Georgio Voice were talking about, nor could he really see their faces. He just knew who they were. Charlie's dad was wearing a sleeveless undershirt and his police uniform slacks, and Georgio Voice had on a blue, pinstripe suit with big lapels like they had back in the 70s. But it wasn't the 70s because Charlie was an adult.

Georgio from the TV said, "I had a second thought about giving you back your gun before you remembered who I was, because when you find out, you'll want to kill me.

"One ball. One strike. A man on third for Oakland."

"You knew me when we were kids. You were about seven. A skinny piece of crap if there ever was one. Didn't give a lick about baseball. All you ever wanted to do was go down to the Belt yards south of Clearing and watch the switchers."

Suddenly, another boy appeared in Charlie's boyhood living room. Seated on the floor in front of the game, he processed a bag of Jay's Potato Chips and either groaned or yelled, "Yes!" when each pitch was thrown. "Strike, two. One and two, runner on third. Batter wants the ump to check the ball."

As impaired by the drug as Charlie was, he began to realize that Georgio's voice wasn't coming from the television; that it was, in fact, Georgio speaking to him. He remembered having been stupid and letting Georgio get the jump on him with the needle, and now he struggled physically and mentally to get out of the lounger, or whatever he sat in, and clear his thoughts. As in any dream, his physical exertion was for naught, and he was unable to free himself from the lounger. The boy on the floor with the bag of chips suddenly turned around to look at him, and Georgio's adult voice came out.

"My name is Georgio Luchesse, and my father was Giannello Luchesse." The boy in the dream giggled a juvenile giggle, as if to telegraph to the struggling boy in the lounger that he had a secret to keep, and then raised his pudgy left hand and pointed to the man at the table with Charlie's father. "Giannello Luchesse," he repeated.

"Don't try to move around too much, Komensky." Georgio's voice sounded real, present, and came to Charlie's ears over highway sounds. Charlie opened his eyes and found that he was seated in the passenger seat of a Subaru zipping along a freeway somewhere in the desert. "You'll hurt yourself."

Rather than panic, Charlie realized that he was experiencing extreme clarity of thought, and decided to go with that. Taking stock of what physical restrictions there may be, he discovered a mildly annoying sore spot at the injection site, and a more annoying bruise under his rib cage on the right. Buckled in loosely, he tried to sit up straight, but found that the sensation of trying to move was much like in the dream. "What the?"

"Easy, Killer. That'll go away soon." Georgio kept his eyes on the road and pressed the gas pedal to pass a double hauler. "What do you remember?"

He found that he remembered quite a few things he had not thought of in years, and that some new ideas about the murders had crystallized. "You and your father."

"Yeah, Charlie. I know. My old man was a heartless killer and he taught me how to survive in a life of crime. I killed him when I was sixteen, and I'm not sorry I did it, because he was beating the shit out of me and it was either him or me. Yadda, yadda. I spent two years in the whole troubled teenager thing and went right back to working for the Italians. You know we ain't got as big a hold as the Russians or the Irish any more.

"I don't want to say that I got a heart of gold or anything, but I do what I can from the inside to see that kids like me have a way out before they have to kill somebody. What else you remember?"

Charlie shifted a little in the seat. His muscles still felt like they were made of lead. "My father." Tears came to his eyes. That wasn't supposed to happen. Charlie Komensky, as a cop, homicide detective, and private eye, had seen and heard lots worse things. "Damn it! My old man was as bad as yours. And Burmeister!"

"Not as bad as mine. Yours didn't smack you around, unless there's something else you remembered that I didn't expect. And Burmeister was a Cook County judge, and a good one. You couldn't stay alive in that job without—let's call it 'compromise.' Yeah, he got your old man involved, and that got him killed. Almost got me killed, too. So I'm just sayin'. For now, we're gonna be on the same side; but I ain't got too many compunctions on blowing the whistle on your buddy Burmeister, either. Dad left me all his stuff, and I'm sure there's something in there an ambitious politico could use to bury a judge, even a retired one."

Charlie now vividly remembered the culmination of that afternoon with the game between Oakland and the Sox blaring from the old TV. Burmeister had told his dad to follow Luchesse's orders, because the judge was about to pass sentence on one of the higher ups in the same crew. Burmeister had decided he wasn't going to get in any deeper, and needed Joe Komensky's help to turn things around.

Then Joe started an argument with Gianello about how the job was to be carried out. The upstart cop made Gianello so furious, that he took it out on Georgio.

In the car, Charlie was able to twist his aching neck just far enough to look at the gangster's face and for the scars that still had to be there. "Why did you have to go back to the life?"

Georgio smiled broadly. "There's the life and there's the life. Testa's not such a bad boss, and he's mostly defanged. Ears pricked up when he heard on the grapevine that the Antwerp stones might be in play. Following you isn't a crime, is it?"

His neck muscles had freed up now, and Charlie started looking around. From what he could gather from the freeway signs, they were in eastern New Mexico and making time due east. "Where are you taking me?"

"I ain't takin' you anywhere. We—you and me—are going to Chicago. You got a text from some guy named Arnie, who says that Walter worked on trains that were ridden by both Dinwiddie and O'Brien, but there was another guy who showed up in the ticketing each and every time, name of Morris Polk, who was ticketed only as far as Kingman. One way, every time."

"So Polk is in Chicago?"

"No. I checked. Nobody knows where Polk is, but he's definitely connected. He did nine cents in solitary after somebody tried to off him—twice, so the story goes—and the cops assigned to the investigation made a case against this guy instead. Guess who his lawyer was."

"Dinwiddie," answered Charlie immediately. This drug, whatever it had been, had put his mind ahead of the story. "So Dinwiddie gets this guy convicted intentionally to keep his contact safe, then starts his own disappearing act. Let me guess again, Polk just got out."

"Better. Before he went bye-bye, he was an import-export jeweler."

Charlie tried to check his watch, and found out it wasn't on his wrist. Georgio saw him struggling, and reached over and opened the console. Charlie's watch, wallet, and .38 appeared intact.

"Your stuff is in the trunk. Wayna Walter is on the train back to Chicago. I don't know how, but he caught up with it in Kingman, about the same time you and me was doin' a little dance back there. He's got friends on the trains, and maybe he feels safe there. I thought you'd like to meet him at Chicago Union Station instead of taking the chance he'll step off somewhere else just to stretch his legs. If we try to board intermediate and spook him, we don't have many other options."

What had before seemed to Charlie to be a jumble of impossibly disconnected facts now seemed perfectly clear. The Indian guide knew too much, and had become the perfect tool for somebody who was really after the remaining diamonds. It had gotten Charlie out of the way for—seeing the date on his watch now—two days. Polk had been involved in moving the diamonds into and through the states, and Dinwiddie and O'Brien, with only indirect criminal ties, had been his couriers. The transfers to the couriers had been made on the train between LA and Kingman, and maybe the stones had even been put aboard by a third henchman—sometime after leaving LA. Somebody had gotten wind of the scheme and either tried to extort Polk, or tried to get him to reveal where the remaining $8 million in diamonds was located. The end users, if they got wind of this, didn't want Polk to spill, so they tried to silence him, first by attempted murder, and then by seeing to it that Dinwiddie got Polk put where he wouldn't be able to talk to anyone for the next 9 years. "Whoever was taking possession of the Antwerp stones in Chicago thought enough of himself that he got over confident. In nine years, he never found out where the remaining stones were located."

Georgio made a sudden lane change and pulled them off the freeway into a dirty little town with a bustling Mobil station and not much else. "Need gas, and you ought to be able to walk now. Go hit the little boy's room before you pee yourself."

When Charlie returned to the car, Georgio was already inside, but he didn't pull right out when Charlie got in. "One thing I don't get."

"Just one?"

"I been workin' for Testa all this time, and you think we woulda heard something about who was rampin' up an assault." He just stared ahead a few seconds, and then hit the gas so hard he squealed the tires all the way back onto the frontage road.

"Want a theory?" offered Charlie.

"You trust me with a theory? I might text it to my boss."

"It wouldn't do him much good. So I think I'll trust you. What you do with it is your business." After a pause while they raced back onto the Interstate at about 90, Charlie said, "You probably know that I tangled with that amazon that got herself popcorned in Chicago. Her crew wasn't local. You probably didn't know that another Euro-felon made a run at me back in northern New Mexico."

"No, I did not."

"So I conclude that the man or woman behind this is a VIP."

"VIP? You mean like some celebrity?"

"No. Northern Euro types, especially around the north coastal areas, use that for Vicious Individual Person. It's someone who would have no compunction about doing whatever it takes to further a criminal enterprise. These types are rumored to be more ruthless than South American drug lords; both feet over the line into some pretty brutal shit. You can tell Testa that, if you want. But I don't have any particular one in mind."

"When we get to our next stop, I'll have one of Angelo's other guys check it out."

They rode the next 70 miles or so in silence, Charlie half wanting to thank Georgio for administering the drug that had cleared up his thinking and half wanting to get the drop on the smug son-of-a-bitch and put him behind bars. Working with Georgio won out by only a narrow margin.

One of the players, the murderer, he assumed, had got Wayna Walter scared enough to stab himself and try to blame Charlie for the deed, risking infection and possibly never being found before the steam locomotive burners were turned on. With or without Georgio's help, Charlie would tail Walter from the station and see what develops. If he could enlist Doug Christie back into the game in the process, he would do so, though he knew Doug would not like Georgio Luchesse being involved. There had to be a payoff for Walter there, real or promised, and that was Walter's likely destination. The Indian had never been east of the Mississippi before.

(OUTSIDE UNION STATION, CHICAGO, THURSDAY, OCTOBER 18, 4:16 P.M. CDT)

Georgio and Charlie took turns driving as fast as they could without attracting attention. They made infrequent food and toilet stops, and arrived outside Chicago Union Station an hour before Walter's train was due in on a cold but clear afternoon. Both men could have used a shave and neither one had the kind of coat to resist 40 degrees with a wind out of the north. It was decided that Charlie would stay with the car and Georgio would text him when he saw Walter come into the concourse from the train. At some point, Walter would have to hail a cab, and Georgio would tell Charlie where to pick him up to follow. It was a risky transition, but they were manpower short. As much as he hated texting, Charlie agreed that it was the only way to go.

Waiting in the Subaru gave Charlie time to think. He liked the way the case was laying itself out, but there was something he couldn't put a finger on still scratching at the back of his brain. Impatient, he picked up his cell phone and punched in Linda's number. He knew she'd caller ID it, and hoped she didn't send it directly to voice mail. But after two rings it picked up. The male voice that answered surprised him so much that whoever it was hung up before he could say anything.

He scrolled up the number and hit send again. The same voice said, "Hello?"

"Is Linda there?"

"Oh, this must be the detective boyfriend. She's indisposed."

"My name's Charlie Komensky, and it's important."

"Well, she's still indisposed. Is there something I can help you with?"

"Who are you?"

"That's impolite, Charlie. You should ask, 'To whom am I speaking?'"

"Are you the fucking accountant?" People correcting Charlie's perfectly good Chicago English was pushing his button for sure. "Sorry, are you that guy Spencer?"

"That's all right, Charlie. I've been called worse. Yes, this is Spencer Dinelli?"

"I just called to make sure Linda is safe."

"Why wouldn't she be safe?"

Charlie didn't like the sound of that. Either it was a truly naïve question or this jerk was playing games with him. "Because she's not returning my calls, and I'm on a case."

"Perhaps, Charlie, it's because you're always on a case that it is I who am here sitting in her living room sipping a mocha macchiato and watching PBS. She's way out of your league, big guy. But you already know that."

He resisted the urge to swear at Dinelli again. "Just tell me she's safe."

"Sure, Charlie. She's safe as long as you don't do something stupid."

"What's that . . . " But Dinelli hung up before Charlie could get it out. "Shit!" He punched in the number Georgio had given him before walking into the station.

"What?" Georgio answered angrily. "I thought we agreed on texting. If somebody spots me and clones this phone."

"I don't know what that means, but I do need to know if Testa has Spencer Dinelli watching Linda."

"You really gotta get with the technology, Komensky; and I don't think so. Dinelli's not on the crew. Angelo doesn't trust him."

"Then we've got problems."

"What! You wanna just leave the Indian go and run off to save your GF who doesn't even want to talk to you? From what I hear, Dinelli is a skirt-chaser from way back. I wouldn't put too much in it."

"Maybe you're right. But once we find out who's meeting Walter, you gotta do me a favor and drive me out to the suburbs."

CHAPTER TWELVE

They had followed the Southside Jiffy Cab to an address on 50th Street, just east of Kimbark, and right down the street from Kenwood Academy. Charlie noted that the neighborhood's appearance had improved some since he'd been a CPD cop; but not so much, he'd wager, that the turf didn't belong to some powerful bad guys. As Charlie got the feel of his immediate surroundings, Georgio filled him in on Walter's actions after getting off the train.

Apparently still struggling with some of the pain from his self-inflicted knife wound, Walter had hauled a heavy duffel bag off the train and up the escalator to street level instead of hailing a cab in the cab court next to the waiting room. He'd passed on at least a dozen cabs before spotting the Jiffy, which came off of Canal street and immediately turned into the curb lane where Walter was standing. Georgio thought it was almost too easy, and somebody had sent the cab, and maybe the diamonds were in the bag. "We'll see," was Charlie's only reaction.

Because the train had been an hour late, darkness had closed in on the neighborhood—no hindrance to Charlie and Georgio, as Chicago's city fathers had never been squeamish about light pollution. They'd parked a half block behind the cab, which was at the curb in front of a frame duplex just a little more dilapidated than most of the rest of the block. Charlie could see the back of the driver's head on the left and the Indian on the right. Neither one seemed in any hurry to get out of the cab. He ordered Georgio to resist jumping out of the Subaru to get closer.

Finally, the driver opened his door, got out, and looked up and down the street. Without saying anything to his fare, the driver closed the door and double-timed to the front door of the duplex. Because of some mature evergreens, Charlie and Georgio lost him at that point. "Okay," said Charlie after some thought. "Maybe they're picking up the contact and going somewhere else."

"Or doing the deal in the cab," Georgio added.

Two minutes went by and nothing happened. Walter hadn't moved and the driver hadn't come back to the cab. Charlie didn't like it. "Something's not right. Get that low-class tail of yours up there and see if you can sneak into the house. I'm going to check on Walter."

After watching Georgio disappear around the side of the house, Charlie checked his .38 and holstered it. He then got out of the car like he belonged in the neighborhood and took the sidewalk until he was just close enough to the cab to be covered by its blind spot. Walter still hadn't moved the whole time, and the street light from just across 50th cast a shadow of Walter's face on the sidewalk next to the cab that spooked Charlie. "Damn son of a bitch!" Pulling a handkerchief from his back pocket, he put it in his left hand to cover prints and quickly strode up to the cab. Gun drawn now in his right hand and ready for Walter, he opened the door. Suspicions confirmed. Walter's corpse sat with a bullet through the chest. Not much blood, signifying a shot through the heart that stopped it immediately. The pattern of burns around the wound said silencer to Charlie. On the front seat of the cab was the duffel, where the driver—or assassin—had gone through it, probably as Charlie and Georgio watched. No diamonds, just clothes and two large Navajo pots for heft. The Indian had followed instructions to frame Charlie, and then to his death.

Before Charlie could think further, he heard an unmistakable gunshot coming from the house. Again taking every precaution, Charlie sprinted to the front door, which he found ajar. Cursing his bad leg as it started to throb with his elevated heart rate, he shoved the door with his foot. The front foyer and living room was empty, but the smell of sulfur and burnt iron hung on the air. Charlie saw light was issuing from the back, illuminating the newly painted walls and woodwork. "Sure," he thought. "This is an unoccupied rehab that some agent probably just listed for sale. Perfect for a clandestine meeting—or murder." He went in ready with the safety off the .38, cleared the foyer and started for the back when he saw the men. Georgio had his gun drawn on a scrawny-looking man with hollow eyes and a gaunt expression. Georgio smiled as Charlie came in, and then looked toward the corner of the dining room, where a third man, the cab driver, was slumped in the corner, one leg out and one leg under him. The bullet Georgio had put between his eyes hadn't even knocked the cab driver's cap off. In the cabbie's right hand was a medium Ruger .22LR with a suppressor. It wouldn't be Charlie's choice for stopping power, but for plugging some poor schmuck passenger from the front seat of your cab, ideal.

"Charlie Komensky," said Georgio before Charlie could check the cabbie for a pulse. "Meet Morrie Polk." The gaunt man smiled sheepishly. "The guy in the corner there was about to put a few rounds into important Polk parts to get Mr. Polk to spill where he's been keeping some diamonds."

"Glad to meet you Mr. Polk. Also glad we all didn't have to witness perforated Polk parts." Charlie, relieved, grinned and rubbed his bad leg. "Luchesse, you know I've got to call CPD. Please turn over your gun."

"Mr. Komensky, sir. You know I can't do that. But here's the deal. I will forgo questioning Mr. Polk myself or conveying his information to Angelo, if you give me ten minutes." Georgio emptied the clip, put the remaining rounds in his pocket, and slammed the empty clip back into the .22. It was then that Charlie realized Georgio was wearing gloves. "This gun belongs to Mr. Polk now." He put the grip firmly into Polk's right hand. "And he knows what's going to happen to him if he says different. Or doesn't cooperate with you.

"Charlie, you're really close now. I think you've got everything you need to find your killer. Why don't you check on our friend over there in the corner." Georgio flicked a light switch just behind his left shoulder, and Charlie looked at the cab driver's body, now illuminated by the dining room chandelier. It was Nick Ramunda, certified international bad guy, the guy from Bernice's cabin.

When Charlie turned back to talk to Georgio, he'd vanished, and Polk just stood there, shaking like an irritated Chihuahua, with a stupid, horrified look on his face. The only thing he could do now is call Doug Christie and hope he picked up.

(CHICAGO POLICE HEADQUARTERS, THURSDAY, OCTOBER 18, 10:35 P.M. CDT)

Surprised that he, too, had not been grilled and made to sign a sworn statement that night, Charlie sat in the outer to Superintendent Aloysius Terwilliger Garrity's inner office at CPD Headquarters reading Morris Polk's signed statement. He still felt as fidgety as a withdrawal symptom as he tried to focus, but at least when he had Doug call Linda she had agreed to come to the phone. With a uniform from RPD headed to her house, it was all he could do for the time being; and he had no real evidence that the accountant was anything worse than a slime ball trying to poach another man's girl.

Polk's statement tied up a lot of loose ends, but really didn't solve the murders, or provide evidence that would put away Angelo Testa, or anyone else. That was going to require more police work. From Terwig's point of view, Charlie had created another mess that couldn't be swept under the rug. By calling Doug instead of police dispatch, Charlie had stepped over the line drawn by Doug when he'd posted bail for Charlie after Bergie the Amazon went all popcorn on him.

Before the scene of Ramunda's untimely demise had been cleared, Doug had told Charlie that Polk had been just a small time fence in LA and sometimes dabbled in finding buyers for stolen property that came into the country with various couriers through LA International. Polk had no history of violent crime, and no known prior associations with any of the known players in the current drama.

In the statement, Polk swore up and down, sideways and standing on his head that he hadn't realized he'd been railroaded into a conviction and put in solitary because of, rather than instead of, the actions of lawyer Dinwiddie. Polk said he got a call about a month after the Antwerp job and was told that he would receive a packet via a German airfreight company that would include three articles and instructions. He never knew who the call came from, and had no knowledge as to whether that call was recorded on any call logs. The packet arrived promptly and contained three Antwerp diamonds with instructions. Polk was to verify the color, cut and clarity of the stones, and authenticate they were actual Antwerp diamonds and had not somehow been pilfered while with the airfreight carrier. Polk was then to cut the diamonds to remove all traces of the Antwerp identification, and then deliver them to a mail drop in the Chicago area.

Polk further stated that the instructions clearly indicated a threat on his life if he failed to make the delivery. Making matters worse, getting caught with the stones, or arrested for any other reason, was to be equally fatal. On the flip side, Polk said he received ten grand for the first delivery of three stones, and, on average, about a grand per rock thereafter. A week after the first three stones were delivered, they started arriving almost daily, with six stones here, four there, a dozen. He stated that he got spooked, and he started looking into the shipping addresses on the packet. Always different, they originated all over Europe. Three days after he started doing an online search, one of the packets showed up empty except for a slip of paper on which was printed, "Curiosity doesn't become you. So don't become curious." After that, he never searched again, nor did he attempt to watch who came to empty the mail drop.

Polk's first derailment came a couple of months into the process, when he was picked for a heightened search by the TSA at LA International. It had dawned on Polk while waiting for the pat down that he was starting to make too many regular flights and was going to get known. Eventually, a diligent TSA officer might become more suspicious despite his jewelry sales credentials. At the same time, some of his contacts in the local underworld had started to get curious why he wasn't buying and selling "local goods" any more.

Knowing that it wouldn't be good for him if local organized crime found out about the windfall, Polk reached out to Dinwiddie, the only real mob contact he knew. For a fee, Dinwiddie was to spread the word that Polk had been visiting a relative in Chicago, but was now back in the game. There would be no more trips to Chicago. Dinwiddie was also to find Polk two or three "couriers" who he could pay to deliver packets of stones to the drop, no questions asked.

Charlie stopped reading and snickered at the inexperience or outright stupidity that Polk evidenced in this statement. Didn't he think the outfit would check to see who the sick relative was? Didn't he think that a courier might eventually turn on him, as one of them obviously had? The statement didn't answer those questions.

Reading on, Charlie learned that Polk was surprised when Dinwiddie showed up a few days later and volunteered to be one of the couriers. He made a quick decision and said yes, as he hadn't made a drop in over a week and worried that his unidentified masters would think he was running out with the loot. Besides, thought Polk, who better than a lawyer who knew how to keep his mouth shut, and who, with mob ties, would be in just as much trouble as Polk if the local wise guys found out? Dinwiddie then quickly put up plastic surgeon O'Brien up for the position of secondary courier, intimating to Polk that the business of providing second rate facelifts for Los Angeles narcissists was not as profitable as one might think, and the supply of criminals needing a face transplant wasn't as plentiful as you might think, either. Thus began the double drops aboard the train, drops that continued until Polk was arrested for securities and tax fraud.

Wayna Walter had been the first and only Amtrak employee to catch on, probably because he had more time on his hands during a trip than the rest of the crew. By necessity, he was taken into their confidence, given a piece of the action, and told that the golden goose would eventually stop laying eggs. All of the three co-conspirators were relative amateurs, and none had the stomach to try to do away with Walter.

When the federal indictment that landed Polk in the joint hit, O'Brien was on a trip with $4 million in stones, street value, and there were about another $4 million left to be delivered kept in a safe deposit box. Polk's bargaining chip for total immunity and maybe even a stint as a protected witness was the number to the personal-access-only box, and the location of the bank that held both keys waiting for Mr. Polk to make that personal access. Polk had rightly never trusted Dinwiddie with this information.

After getting out of prison, Polk had neither time nor inclination to go to the safe deposit box. Before he could get situated in an apartment—his old house in Van Nuys had been torn apart by the feds and auctioned by the mortgage company—he started to hear from his old contacts. The criminal community was abuzz that Antwerp diamonds were coming into play. Unable to reach either Dinwiddie or O'Brien, Polk had called Walter and arranged to meet in Chicago. Nothing in Polk's statement admitted to giving Walter instructions to frame Charlie. Charlie had been right! Walter had a good reason to be afraid, but it was afraid of someone else!

A shiver went up Charlie's spine as he heard the door to Terwig's office open. Terwig and Doug Christie walked out along with Terwig's chief of staff, a young, ambitious and poorly trained political appointee named Sveltheimer. Terwig wore his usual scowl like it was sown on, and neither Doug nor the diminutive chief of staff, whose Sears Best suit hung on him like a grey shroud, looked happy. Charlie decided not to get up and kept reading.

"Don't ignore me, Komensky! And that's an order!" growled Terwig as he parked his imposing presence in front of the chair where Charlie sat.

"Not ignoring, Chief. Just catching up. This Polk is quite a catch for you, sir. Might lead to CPD getting the credit for solving a big, international crime."

Terwig looked like he was going to bite a lip off. "You have a bad habit of buttering both sides of the bread, Komensky."

Charlie stood up and put the file on the side table. "Just saying."

"Charlie," offered Doug in a conciliatory tone. "I've just been telling Superintendent Garrity and CS Sveltheimer that we're all on the same side. They want to hear from you, if you can mind your manners long enough to tell them how you see this going down."

"Really?" Charlie crooked a finger at Doug to listen more closely. "The only way I'm going to share is if the glorified steno goes away and we agree that I'm not the bad guy here." They looked at Terwig for an answer.

Terwig addressed his CS. "How are we on press coverage?"

"The press hasn't got this one yet, sir," answered Sveltheimer in a nasal voice that reminded Charlie of something from a Fox animated series. "Time and location were in our favor. And there's that gang rape thing in Rogers Park."

Terwig looked back at Doug, and then at Charlie, and then he sighed deeply. It even evoked some sympathy in Charlie, who knew Terwig was fighting national press reports that pictured Chicago as the 21st Century Murder Capitol times ten. Finally, Terwig said, "Okay, get the hell out of here and see to it that they don't, or I'll know that these men are right not to trust you. I don't want to see your ass back in my office until I send you an invitation. Got it?"

The CS headed out to the corridor without a word, leaving the ball in Charlie's court. Okay, so be it. "What are the ballistics on the Ruger .22 that killed Walter?"

"Heh, heh. You don't waste time, Komensky. Maybe you should have Sveltheimer's job."

"You're stalling, Chief!" snapped Charlie. "Besides, the first thing I'd do is tell the press to go to Hades."

Terwig worked his jaw a few seconds, and then answered the question. "Nothing. We got nothing. The gun was not used to murder Dr. O'Brien and isn't in the system."

"What about the drop in the suburbs where they were delivering the diamonds?"

"Cook County's working on it. The address given for the box rental was a dead end on the southwest side of Chicago. The house is empty and the last resident was an old lady who is now in a senior center. The name and social were bogus. The box has been rented so many times since the drops that prints are useless. Officer Christie? Is there anything I've forgotten?"

His confidence restored, Charlie figured Doug would share everything one way or the other, so was not concerned when Doug shook his head no. Charlie then addressed Terwig: "The way I see it is the only crime committed in your jurisdiction is the murder of Wayna Walter"

"I'm taking your word for that." Terwig looked like the wind had been knocked out of him.

"Don't worry," consoled Charlie. "You'll have more than one witness by the time this thing's all over."

Charlie then went on to lay out the rest for Doug and Terwig. "The only way CPD is going to come out with some points on this one is we arrest the murderer of O'Brien and Dinwiddie for my clients and then we pinch the man behind the Antwerp robbery.

"Those ain't necessarily the same person," he went on. "But they could be. First, there's the person, call him Person One, who let it be known that the diamonds were coming back into play on Polk's release from prison. That information alone would have been enough to mobilize a dozen possible suspects with the means to fence those stones. Person One had to know that timing this for Polk's release from solitary and into the real world put eveyone's eyes on Polk and make his survival less likely. Person One also had to know that there were $4 to $8 million in diamonds undelivered, so Person One is either one of the original robbers or the original buyer.

"Then there's Person Two. Like Person One, he wants to stir things up, but decides to take action. Person Two would have to know that O'Brien was the last courier, and would have to be the murderer. To place an Antwerp stone, he would have to have some, or have made O'Brien talk, revealing the location of any remaining stones from his delivery, before being killed. The stone Cook County found on O'Brien was a message to Polk, or to anyone else looking, that Person Two was a serious contender. Putting the body into a steam train was either a clue to who Person Two is, or a warning that Person Two knew how the stones were being delivered."

Doug Christie broke in. "But then there would have been no reason to kill Dinwiddie."

"Oh, yes, there is. There are two reasons, actually." Charlie started holding up fingers. "One: O'Brien only knew where his stash was, not where Polk kept the rest of them. Two: Dinwiddie was killed just to involve me."

Both Terwig and Doug Christie seemed shocked by this deduction, so Charlie said, "Yeah, that's kind of paranoid, isn't it?"

Terwig seemed to have lost the scowl and was now truly interested in what Charlie had to say. He asked a door-opening question. "What do you propose we do to find Persons One and Two."

"Simple. You get the feds to promise Polk immunity and a new identity, and Polk gives us the location of the last $4 million in diamonds. When we get them here to CPD, safe and sound, Polk does us one last favor: We pretend to let him loose, and he leads us to a hiding place of our choosing, where we wait until our suspect or suspects show up. We wire him up and down and make sure that we have an eye in the sky. Leave nothing to chance."

"What if they don't show up."

"Then you've recovered $4 million in property for its rightful owner, and the perps will have to wait for another day. But they'll show."

Doug's cell phone lit up and buzzed like a sex toy with a bad battery, and he hit the little lock icon on the screen and picked up. "This is Christie." His face fell. "Shit!" This wasn't good, and Charlie already knew it. Doug held up two fingers and then started giving directions. "Get a warrant, if you have to, but get inside there."

Charlie snatched the phone from Doug and barked at the caller. "This is Charlie Komensky and the possible victim is Linda Chelwood. She's the homeowner and she's very close to me. Tell me you get it." There was a pause. "Good. The Riverside chief owes me from my days with Berwyn PD, so forget the warrant and get in there and make sure she's not in there somewhere bleeding to death. You get it? Good." He hit the disconnect button, gave the phone back to Doug, and then said to nobody in particular, "Whole game's changed now."

CHAPTER THIRTEEN

(CHARLIE'S OLD NEIGHBORHOOD, CHICAGO, SATURDAY, OCTOBER 20, 9:12 A.M. CDT)

Deciding he was tired of dealing with police departments that had more moles than a Greek nudist, Charlie needed some leverage that would put his fate, and Linda's, back into his own hands. It wasn't a formal kidnapping case yet, and by morning it was clear to him that the inertia of uninspired police work had determined that his girlfriend could just as easily have been spooked by Doug's call and taken off for a vacation rather than deal with another one of Charlie's messed up cases. Her car and keys were gone, her purse was gone, and there was no sign of violence. Maybe she just forgot to lock the front door.

That's not how things worked in Charlie's world. In Charlie's world—even truer now that he knew about Judge Burmeister and the Italian mob—favors got done or reminder notices got sent out. Linda disappearing was a reminder notice: Bill due or subject to late penalties.

"Why here?" Judge Burmeister exhaled into his hands to keep warm. They stood on the sidewalk in front of Joe Komensky's old house at 62nd Street and Menard Avenue. The weather had turned into a typical Chicago overcast, with a cloud layer so thick that no sun position could be determined, and so uniformly, unremittingly gray that the overcast itself could be just inches above the rooftops of the neat rows of bungalows and two-flats and you wouldn't have known it. Many times, on fall days like this, a young Charlie Komensky had stood at the west fence of Midway airport, just a few blocks to the east, and not been able to see the five miles or so to the Sears Tower. The weather felt like Charlie's mood, cold and persistent, even though he had already extracted so many favors from Burmeister that he should have been overjoyed at the progress. The blessing of connections with federal and state judges all over the country had clamped a lock on Polk's confession and a restraint on any further action by CPD. The miracle of private jet paid for by the Antwerp Diamond Exchange would deposit $4 million in diamonds on the tarmac at Midway in a couple of hours.

Charlie had managed to get home and get some fitful sleep before dressing in a blue broadcloth shirt and the cleanest pair of Dockers and throwing on his heavier leather jacket and jumping on the bus. His old Taurus wouldn't start after being ignored for three weeks. "I could say it's close to the airport."

"But you're not." Judge Burmeister snugged up his tweed overcoat, adjusted his gray wool newsboy hat, and stuffed his hands in his pockets. "So why did you want to meet here?"

"Isn't this where we all go to lie to each other?"

"I've never lied to you."

Charlie took a step closer, just into the trail of steam from the judge's breath. The bags under the judge's eyes looked more pronounced in the flat light; his age lines, too. "Oh, you just omitted some important stuff." He knew he was taking a chance. The judge could shut him down in a heartbeat, but he had to get it all out before the rest of this case played out. The accusation in his voice cut the cold air like a hot wire. "So you just felt so guilty that you got my father killed that you been doing me all these favors. Did you start screwing my mother before or after?"

"I . . . I loved your mother," stammered the judge. "After . . . you know. Afterwards, you didn't seem to know . . . or care, so I hoped I'd never have to have this conversation."

"A little bird named Luchesse helped me remember." Charlie suddenly realized the his bad leg was aching him in the cold, and he longed for the euphoria he had felt after Georgio's truth drug. "Remember Luchesse?"

"Georgio wasn't supposed to say anything."

"Another favor? Was it for him or for Testa?"

"Charlie! For God's sake, don't ruin things. Georgio's a good man. I've kept an eye on him, and we're getting things done. With him on the inside, and my contacts, we're making inroads. We're fighting and winning."

"And my father was the first casualty of the war?"

Judge Burmeister hung his head for a second, then looked Charlie in the eye. "In a way, your father has helped more than anyone else. I learned a lot of things from that disaster. Things I've put to use since. I was a little less than your age now back then."

In no mood to be lectured, or lied to again, Charlie just asked, "Yeah, like what?"

"Well, for one thing, doing all this out in the open is going to get somebody killed. Since your dad, I've tried to avoid that."

"Nothing ventured," said Charlie, unable to avoid sneering in the process.

The black SUV that came around the corner and pulled to the curb adjacent to them radiated FBI like a skunk radiated stink. Judge Burmeister flashed his ID at the agent in the passenger seat, who got out and opened the curb side rear. Just as Charlie had instructed, the agent in the back seat with Polk pushed the jeweler out the side door so hard that he almost face-planted in the dry grass, and the "unmarked" drove off with a squeal of tires. They now had a clandestine meeting with an ex judge and a federal suspect, who had been mysteriously and unceremoniously released from custody.

The trip in Burmeister's own SUV to the west side of Midway took only a few minutes, during which time Charlie filled the frightened Polk in on what was to happen. Charlie's only hope was that Burmeister still felt guilty enough to go along with the plan completely. If Charlie couldn't rely on police assistance, then he could use emotional blackmail as well as the rest.   At the west gate, the judge used his credentials again to get them past TSA. The jet landed on schedule, a medium sized ten-seater with no markings other than the registration number, again as Charlie had requested. Charlie checked to make sure the whole process was visible from outside the gate, and they made a big show of collecting the stones, held in a small cloth case about the size of a mini-laptop, from the two guards on board. Charlie even went so far as to make it look like money was changing hands, although the only thing he gave the guards was a bag of cold fast food.

Back on the road again, about half way to downtown from the airport on the Stevenson Expressway, Burmeister checked his rearview. "We've got two, maybe three following us."

"What!" exclaimed Polk.

Charlie turned to calm him. "This is expected. Look, Mr. Polk, you're wearing a wire and there's about a dozen federal agencies listening in. Just make it look like you're working with me."

Polk was visibly shaking. "For a minute there, I thought you were going lone wolf."

"It's good that it looks that way. Now let's just hope at least one of these tails we've got has Linda in the back seat."

Six blocks from the lake, at the Chicago River bridge for Jackson Boulevard, and just outside the entrance to the Amtrak station, the overcast had dropped to surface fog, and the visibility shortened to about a block. Charlie had had Judge Burmeister drop him and Polk east of the river, and Charlie's abrupt reason was given as, "I don't want to feel the same kind of guilt if you get killed." To their tails, it would look like they were taking a train out of town with the diamonds.

With the bag under his left arm, Charlie and Polk walked silently until they got to the west end of the bridge. Beneath the bridge, about 70 feet below, the dark river lapped at pilings and made barely visible swirls of scum mixed with general urban debris. These accumulated at the edges of the concrete wall that formed the west shore of the river and kept it from flooding the train station. Charlie had always marveled at the engineering that allowed magnificent architecture with vast, underground facilities to coexist with the old river and the sixty to eighty feet of wet Chicago clay that underpinned the city. From here, Charlie could look above the water's edge and the concrete wall, through concrete columns, and into the track level of the station. The old station and tracks had long ago been surmounted by office buildings. A promenade ran parallel to the river on the same level as the bridge and disappeared to the north into the gloom before it got to the next bridge at Adams Street. On a sunny weekday, pedestrian traffic would have been heavy; but this was a gloomy Saturday, and only a handful of people chose the exposed promenade over the warm shop-lined passages through the buildings. At this time of year, pleasure boats would be mostly moored or stored, but Charlie identified the sound of at least one motorized watercraft somewhere in the fog north of them. He couldn't tell if it was approaching or not.

Charlie gave Polk a look that was meant to keep him in line, but the expression on Polk's pasty face was nothing other than submission and dismay. They'd been there twenty minutes when Charlie spotted two men in dark jackets walking toward them from the west, one of whom was Georgio Luchesse and the other presumably Angelo Testa. Testa looked younger and thinner than Charlie would have guessed from the mug shots he'd seen. He wore a battered felt hat and casual dark slacks. As he came closer, Charlie could see the porcine nose that he'd noticed in some of those jailhouse shots as well as the sad eyes and thin lips. Testa's complexion was pale, with only a hint of color just above the cheekbones, and he had cultivated a short goatee that hadn't appeared in any of his earlier photos. Polk reacted to seeing Georgio, as Charlie had expected, so Charlie whispered, "Stand your ground."

Georgio's boss walked right up to Charlie and Polk, who had their backs to the large concrete corner post that marked the connection between the bridge railing and the promenade. Georgio, on the other hand, held back a little so that he was behind and to Testa's right. "Charles Komensky. I hope you liked your visit to my model train room." Testa spoke with a South Chicago accent overlaid with a hint of Italian. Without waiting for an answer, Testa stated, "And this is Morris Polk."

Remembering his coaching, Polk spoke up. "And you must be the brains behind the Antwerp diamond heist, and the guy that got me locked up for 8 years."

Taking the bait, Testa started to talk, but caught himself. "Before we talk about my, shall we say, accomplishments, why don't you tell me how you expected to get away with blowing town with $8 million of somebody else's property."

Polk stayed on it. "You just did the robbery, but I did time for this stuff. You owe me."

Charlie added, "You owe us."

Testa shrugged his shoulders and relaxed a little. "If I owe, I'll pay you. Angelo Testa always pays his debts. And, for the record, I didn't have nothin' to do with that robbery, and you and your errand boys never delivered a single thing to me. That was my brother."

"There was never anybody named Testa on the list of possible suspects," Charlie improvised, hoping to get a name.

Testa chuckled. "I bet you got a A in interrogation, Komensky. My worthless brother fucked up that job. Last time I knew he was in a Marseille jail."

Charlie had done his homework in the time available before meeting Burmeister that morning, and knew that no Testa had been jailed in France, or anywhere on the European continent in the last five years. "But I'll tell you this," Testa went on. "I've got a recorded confession from the little shit, and I'm going to use it to get my hands on whatever this stinkin' shit of a jeweler actually did deliver to him." Testa glowered menacingly at Polk, who shrank back. At the same time, the gangster pulled a small caliber, silver plated pistol from under his jacket and pointed it at Charlie. "Give."

Charlie's eyes met Georgio's, and, without missing a beat, the former goon did his one-step with the needle. Testa went limp, and Georgio deftly made it appear that he was assisting his slightly under the weather boss to the bench next to the station entrance. Two strands of heavy cable tie quickly assured Testa was benched for the duration.

Thinking everything was over, Polk almost fainted, but steadied himself against the concrete corner. Georgio stood up from this cable tying, but before he could walk back to the two men, a voice called from the promenade north of them. "Notarbartolo is Testa's brother." The voice belonged to Nate Steinmetz.

Luchesse pulled out his new gun, this time a quite adequate .45 revolver with a long barrel, but Charlie shook his head and the ex-goon put it back under his jacket. From the fog emerged Steinmetz walking arm in arm with Linda Chelwood in a close hold that made it clear to Charlie that Nate had a gun under his overcoat aimed at Linda's right side, just under the rib cage and pointing upward. That kind of bullet delivered at close range would make a nasty, unrecoverable wound. "Mr. Charles," said Nate as he brought Linda to a halt just out of arm's reach. "I believe you have something that belongs to me, and I have something that belongs to you."

Charlie looked into Linda's eyes and saw what he always knew about her: Yes, she would fear for her life, but she would never let a bad situation get her so rattled that she wasn't thinking clearly. Her blue eyes sparkled, ready for action, ready to take cue's from Charlie. "She doesn't belong to me anymore," Charlie stated flatly. "We split."

"Charles, Charles." Nate's tone was harder than Charlie had ever heard it. "I have already dispatched a lawyer and a *goyisher kop* doctor for being dishonest with me. I think your *shiksa* would expect more from you, wouldn't you, darling?" Linda tensed up until Nate jabbed her a little with the unseen weapon. It looked like she'd taken only a light fall coat with her, and it wasn't offering any protection from the jabs or from the cold wind that blew constantly down river without parting the persistent fog. "You will lay the case at my feet while I hold this gun on your *zaftige* whore. After which I will fade away into the fog."

"It was you that Polk was delivering the diamonds to, wasn't it?"

"That is water under the bridge; a fitting metaphor for where we now stand, Mr. Charles."

"You were the only one who could have known my mother's old address when you rented the drop box." Charlie had recognized the address as his mother's when the investigating officer had not.

"Spilled milk! Sour wine! Now do it!"

"How you gonna get away, Nate?" Charlie nodded towards Georgio, who was still ready to draw his gun at a snap. "You're a fat old man, and you don't run so good anymore, Nate."

"Perhaps I have friends on the building across the river. With guns."

"The fog's too thick."

Nate laughed. "Would you care to test that?"

But Charlie didn't have to. Without warning, Polk shouldered Charlie, grabbed the case from under his arm, and, surprising Nate, went running north on the promenade. Nate let go of Linda, turned and leveled his gun at Polk's back. Before he could squeeze off a shot, Linda swung around, pushed herself hard off the concrete railing, and gave Nate one of her best kick-boxing moves right between the shoulder blades. The fat jeweler grunted and went down like a sack of beets, his .357 clattering under the railing and falling into the river. No one shot at them from across the river. "I think we tested it," quipped Charlie as Georgio started after Polk.

Charlie had two more cable ties at the ready, and Georgio had taken no more than three strides when they both saw the muzzle flashes through the gloom. The reports echoed several times off the many tall buildings across the river, and then the nasal voice of Polk groaned in obvious agony, "Aughhh! What? Who the hell are you."

"Will you be okay?" asked Charlie, as he left Linda to run into the fray.

"Don't do anything stupid," she warned with a sly smile. "You never know when some *zaftige* whore is going to need rescuing."

Both Charlie and Georgio caught sight of Polk first. He was staggering toward them and bleeding profusely from a massive hole in his left side, then he went down. "Georgio, see if you can stop the bleeding," ordered Charlie. There was no time to think about it, and he just ran forward up the promenade and into the gloom.

He caught sight of the huge figure of a man in a long riding coat, holding a micro Uzi, and standing on one of the pilasters between sections of railing. "Stop," yelled Charlie with leveled gun. The huge man looked in his direction. Notarbartolo!

The robber fired a burst in Charlie's direction, causing him to roll for cover. By the time he came up, Notarbartolo was disappearing over the top of the pilaster.

Running to the railing, Charlie looked over, but couldn't see where the man had gone. Running forward again, he stopped every few steps to look over. The fog over the river was just too thick. Maybe Notarbartolo had somehow gotten over the wall into the station. Should he attempt a foot chase? It would take him two or three minutes just to get down to that level, over two escalators or three flights of stairs, and God knew he was in no shape to try to climb down the decorative work from the outside with his bad leg.

Georgio walked up from behind him shaking his head. The jeweler didn't make it. It was then that they both heard the unmistakable sound of a launch down on the river and heading toward the turning basin, and they knew that Notarbartolo had gotten away.

(HOME OF AGATHA AND DOUG CHRISTIE, CHICAGO, SUNDAY, OCTOBER 21, 6:00PM CDT)

"I don't know how you do it, but you always get me involved in these shoot 'em ups of yours even when I don't want to talk to you." Linda chided. She and Charlie were seated on one side of the table. Doug Christie, at the head, ladled out a big helping of Aggie's Irish stew into Charlie's bowl. Superintendent Garrity and Aggie occupied the two spaces opposite, and the sixth place at the Christie table was unoccupied. The house, furnished with some traditional Irish decorations and some secondhand furniture befitting a cop's salary, felt warm and homey.

"Where's your new mob buddy?" asked Doug, taking up the needling.

Terwig wiped a big smear of stew off his face with a napkin and added, "They were childhood sweethearts."

Charlie looked around at all the smiling faces. "Yeah, yeah! If he didn't pick this case to go straight on, you'd be tearing me a new one over something else. So you guys just keep talking and I'll keep eating. Aggie, did I tell you this stuff is addictive?"

"Every time you come over, Charlie. So what's going on with the big European Mafioso?"

Charlie welcomed the change in subject and was glad that his new old friend hadn't accepted the dinner invitation. This way, he wouldn't have to skirt the truth about Judge Burmeister and the mob connections between Joe Komensky and Giannello Luchesse. "Judge B was able to get DHS and the FBI on alert. Unfortunately, there's over three hundred miles of riverfront in Chicago, and with that fog the other day, satellite was useless."

"Some security camera will pick him up," interjected Doug. "He's a pretty big guy. Not that he got away with anything."

Terwig spoke with his mouth full. "Except for discharging a firearm without proper authority in the City of Chicago, witness tampering, murder." Silence followed. "What? I'm serious."

Aggie broke the awkward moment. "Speaking of murder, what will happen to your friend Nate?"

"I should have known he was involved when he came up with all that info on Antwerp and Notarbartolo. And it doesn't say much for my ability to spot clues when they're right in front of my face." Charlie took time to wash down a mouthful of stew.

"What did you miss?" asked Doug.

"A picture on Nate's office wall that showed he had been in the Israeli Army Medical Corps. The Heil HaRfu'a. They use injection guns extensively in the Middle East. And his shoes. Who would be more likely to take their shoes to a shoemaker than a thrifty Jewish shopkeeper! You will remember that our New Mexico murderer had shoes with new soles. But there was another clue; not an obvious one. The cops in San Bernardino knew they had taken an expensive stone off me, but didn't connect it to Antwerp. It had already been cleaned by Polk, although I didn't know it at the time." Charlie sighed as if sad. "So Nate was full of it when he told me the diamond was still marked, and my formerly trusted friend will stand trial for murder in California and New Mexico, and then answer to federal kidnapping charges and assault charges in Illinois."

Doug tried to change the subject by asking, "Didn't CPD pick up the accountant this afternoon, Chief Garrity?"

"Yes, we did. And don't think I don't know that you guys all call me Terwig." Doug and Charlie gave each other knowing looks, and then they all broke out in laughter. "It's just a shame that Testa will probably get a good lawyer and get off in return for fingering his estranged brother. Looks like brother Testa got himself adopted by an American couple and got a new name before he hooked up with the outfit. That's why we didn't connect the two. Brother Notarbartolo just went bad using the old, family name."

After the bowls were cleared and a pot of tea and plate of scones put on the table, Aggie restarted the conversation and went straight back to the case. "There's just one thing I don't understand. Were the electrocuted woman and the Belgian assassin working for Testa, his brother, or Nate?"

"I got this one," answered Charlie. "The woman called Bergie gave me another hint when she told me there was something more about me than just that I took the diamond from the New Mexico victim. That tells me she was hired by Nate Steinmetz. If she ever gets out of rehab, maybe we can confirm that. As for Ramunda, we'll have to ask Notarbartolo, when we get him."

"You may not," noted Terwig. "If he tries to sell those fake diamonds to anyone, they just might take him out."

Linda, who had been mostly quiet, exclaimed, "You mean you . . . ?"

"Safe and sound in a California bank." Charlie smiled at her.

"I think that Bergie had the hots for you," said Doug, changing the tone to jabbing Charlie again. "A girl in every port."

Charlie turned to Linda to see if this would hurt her. "Are we okay, Doll? I mean really okay?"

"Charlie Komensky, if you pull out another piece of shrapnel and try to put it on my finger to match this piece of tin. . ." She held up her finger with the makeshift engagement ring Charlie had made after his last big case. "I swear I'll slit your throat with it."

He held up both hands, palms forward. That Linda still wore the faux engagement ring said volumes to him. He almost got up to hug her, but then decided not to push it. Instead, he said, "When my big reward check comes in from the Antwerp Diamond Exchange, then we'll talk."

CHARLIE KOMENSKY'S STEAM LOCOMOTIVE GLOSSARY

- **AIR** – generally referring to the air held on reserve in the brake system for stopping the engine. Dumping the air results in an emergency stop.
- **ATOMIZER** – steam driven device for adding air and steam to fuel oil for more efficient combustion
- **BACKHEAD** – back of the boiler.
- **BOILER** – the part of the locomotive where water is heated to make steam to drive the cylinders.
- **BOILER EXPLOSION** – what happens when water gets too low causing failure of a boiler component, usually a crownsheet or flue, that results in release of boiler pressure and instantaneous conversion of all superheated water to steam of a volume far in excess of the total volume of boiler available.
- **CAB** – where the engineer and fireman sit or stand when they run the locomotive.
- **COMPOUND** or cross-compound pumps – Steam operated air compressor pumps used to create braking air.

- **CROWNSHEET** – steel sheet, part of the boiler over the fire and firebox. Water in the boiler must always cover the crownsheet to prevent explosion.
- **CYLINDERS** – steam is directed into these to push pistons and drive the driving wheels through rods. Steam engines reciprocate and drive the pistons from both sides through a valve gear arrangement. Valve cylinders may sit on top of the piston cylinders.
- **DERAIL** – a device set on the track against the possible movement of the locomotive, especially one with a leaky throttle, to derail it before it rolls onto an active track or into the path of another train. Derails are sometimes built into the track. At other times, they are portable and can be clamped to the track where needed.
- **DRIVE RODS** or **MAIN RODS** (sometimes **SIDE RODS**) – the large rods that convert the push and pull of the pistons to rotary motion of the wheels.
- **DRIVE WHEELS** – the wheels connected to the drive rods and moved by them to move the locomotive.
- **FEEDWATER HEATER** – steam operated appliance for pre-heating water before it is injected into the boiler.
- **FIRE DOOR** – door on the back of the boiler that can be opened to view the fire or provide fuel.
- **FLUE** or **BOILER TUBE** – tube running through the middle part of the boiler to carry hot gasses for more efficient heating of boiler water. Most locomotives have many flues or tubes.
- **INJECTOR** – steam operated appliance for injecting, or adding cold water to the boiler.
- **JOURNAL BOX** – boxlike casting covering wheel bearings on old railroad equipment with a door on the

outside and usually filled with oil and oil soaked cotton fabric to maintain lubrication on old style friction bearings. The extension of the axle into the journal box is the journal.

- **OIL CUPS** – places on or in the side rods where oil can be put for lubrication of bearings.
- **OIL PUMP** – this can be a pump to move fuel oil from the tender to the firebox on oil fired locomotives and also a mechanical appliance operated from the valve or rod motion to lubricate wear points or bearings on the locomotive.
- **PILOT** or **PILOT DECK** – sometimes referring to the pony truck, but actually the track level front of the locomotive, colloquially the cowcatcher, and the front extension of the engine frame forming a platform below and in front of the smokebox door.
- **PONY TRUCK** – non-driven front wheels and axle(s) that partially support the weight of smokebox and cylinder castings. Proper suspension on this kind of truck also guides the locomotive into curves.
- **REVERSER** – a lever or screw, sometimes with a pneumatic assist (called power reverser) that sets the valve motion to forward or reverse, and also adjusts the valve gear to use steam efficiently by cutting off before a full stroke of the piston in the cylinder.
- **SAND DOME** – storage atop the boiler where sand is kept warm and dry for producing traction on slippery rails.
- **SMOKEBOX** – chamber on the front of the boiler where hot smoke and gasses mix with steam before going up the stack.

- **SMOKEBOX DOOR** – access door on the front of the smokebox to be used only when the engine is cold.
- **STACK** – a chimney positioned on the smokebox above the cylinders where hot gasses of combustion and steam escape into the atmosphere.
- **STEAM DOME** – part of the boiler where steam is collected for delivery to the cylinders.
- **STEAM ENGINE** – term used to describe the entire locomotive; but technically just the cylinders, drive wheels, and associated rods and valve gear.
- **STEAM LINE** – piping on the locomotive, tender, and any other cars that may have or convey steam to appliances (such as heating and cooling) for passenger amenities. Modern passenger cars use power generated by diesel driven alternators or generators for these purposes, and, in general, do not need steam lines.
- **STOKER** – steam operated device for moving coal from a tender to the firebox for combustion.
- **SUPERHEATER** – piping used to carry steam back through the flues to be heated above the boiling point resulting in superheated steam that contains more energy for pushing the pistons and moving the engine than steam at the boiling temperature of water.
- **TENDER** – the car usually pulled behind the locomotive with supplies of fuel and water for the trip. A tender usually has a larger volume of water than of fuel.
- **THROTTLE** – generally, the control in the locomotive cab that the driver or engineer uses to regulate the movement of the locomotive. Specifically, in a steam locomotive, a valve controlled by a throttle lever and mechanical or pneumatic linkage that allows steam to

flow from the boiler to the cylinders in a regulated manner.

- **TRAILING TRUCK** – usually non-driven rear wheels and axle(s) that partially support the weight of the boiler, firebox, and cab and may provide rearward guidance. Trailing trucks may also be powered by auxiliary steam engines.

- **TURBO-GENERATOR** – a steam operated appliance usually sitting on top of the locomotive firebox and used to make low voltage, direct current for lighting. Steam locomotives do not generate electricity for any cars they pull. Sometimes more generally: dynamo.

- **VALVE GEAR** – an arrangement of cranks and rods that are moved by the drive wheels and are adjustable to direct steam to the proper place in the cylinders at the proper time. Controlled by a reverser or reverse lever or crank.

www.ingramcontent.com/pod-product-compliance
Lightning Source LLC
Chambersburg PA
CBHW070617130626
46556CB00001B/395